THE BLOOD STAIN

KAYLA N. DEMPSEY

Order this book online at www.trafford.com
or email orders@trafford.com

Most Trafford titles are also available at major online book retailers.

Printed in the United States of America.

ISBN: 978-1-4669-8048-8 (sc)
ISBN: 978-1-4669-8047-1 (e)

Trafford rev. 03/26/2013

 www.trafford.com

North America & international
toll-free: 1 888 232 4444 (USA & Canada)
phone: 250 383 6864 ♦ fax: 812 355 4082

Dedication

This book is dedicated to my dad and mom
and my two best friends, Juwan and Jalyn.

Introduction

Ever since my best friend found out what I was, she has been too scared to get near me. No matter how much I try to explain to her. She just will not listen. No one will.

I never meant for her to find out, it just, kind of, happened. She walked in on me right after I had attacked a squirrel and was sucking its blood. I turned and saw her standing there. I felt the warm blood running down my chin. She turned and ran.

I don't think she has told anyone. No one has asked me anything. I think she fears people will say she has gone crazy. That vampires are not real. But she saw me, she knows the truth. No one can change her mind.

But I am not the type of vampire that attacks people. I just attack small animals. But I can't deny that sometimes I am tempted, but I never attack. Most vampires do attack humans, but that's the bad kind.

Well anyway, there's a new kid at school, his name is Ryan. He's supposed to come to my school tomorrow, which is the first day for everyone else too. I just hope he isn't one of the preppy kind of guys. I hate them. They think they're so perfect and better than everyone else. I would love to teach them a lesson, but I don't want everyone to know I am a vampire. Everyone believes the preps. No matter what they say.

But still, it would be good for them to see how it feels to be on the other end of the food chain. Then maybe they'd cut out the stupid stuff they do, like embarrassing people for their entertainment.

Anyway, as I was saying I hope this Ryan kid isn't like that. Maybe he is a vampire too; maybe I will finally have someone who understands.

I mean, I haven't told anyone about my being a vampire, not even my parents. The only person that knows is Karla, my best friend

I mentioned earlier, and that's it. I don't want anyone else to know, I never wanted Karla to know, but you can't change what's already happened, can you?

Plus, maybe this happened for a reason; maybe Karla was supposed to know. Maybe she could help me. If she ever talked to me again. I mean, if she hadn't told anyone maybe she was trying to protect me, trying to make sure nobody else found out, like a true friend.

She found out a couple months ago. I'm sure the shock must wear off sometime, I hope. Maybe, since tomorrow was the first day of school, she would talk to me again. She might have thought about it over the summer and realized I need her now more than ever.

I would find out if Karla is still my friend and if this Ryan kid was what I hoped he was tomorrow. I had a weird feeling that I was right about the new kid being a vampire, and an even weirder feeling that I was going to like it.

Or maybe the weird feeling was just a desire to have a friend who was exactly like me in every way. Someone who knows what it's like to have this annoying thirst for blood that makes everyone who knows afraid to come too close. And everyone who knows doesn't want to be friends with you anymore because they think you are a killer.

CHAPTER 1
First Day

First day of school. Fun. At least I was able find out more about the new kid. And maybe Karla would talk to me. A lot of things happen over the summer. Like some, but not all, preps try to deprep themselves to become normal but never stick to it. And the geeks try to become preps but go back to what they really are. Then there is my social status: the normals. Well, I never had any friends outside of my status group.

And today was judgment day. For the new kid anyway, because once you are placed in a group there was no getting out of it.

So I was sitting at my usual table, when I saw him: the new kid. He was a couple inches shorter than me with golden brown hair, and pretty sea blue eyes. And he was walking straight towards the prep tables. I wanted to warn him, but the status rules forbid it. I was left to just watch and hope for the best. He sat down. Judgment time.

"Why are you sitting here?" I heard one of the preps shout.

"Yeah, who said a normal could sit at our table?" shouted another.

So he was like me. He was in the same status. If only he was a vampire then we would really be the same.

"You're supposed to sit over there." shouted the first prep, pointing at the empty seat beside me, which was usually filled by Karla.

So Ryan got up and walked over to the seat he was appointed, right beside me, and sat. He did not say or do anything, just sat.

The bell rang. Everyone but him packed up and went to class. When he realized I was still there and looking at him. He turned away, but still sat there. So I spoke up.

"Do you need help getting to your classes?" I asked. That was so pathetic, but at least I didn't ask, 'are you a vampire', that would be suspicious. But his answer was normal as if he didn't know how pathetic it was.

"Yes, please. If you have enough time." he said. He turned toward me and handed me his schedule.

I looked at the schedule. I had seen it before. Then I realized that he had the exact same schedule as me.

"You have the same classes as me; it shouldn't be too hard." I joked.

"Thanks." he laughed.

I gathered my stuff, and he did the same. He looked sad. But I don't think he wanted me to notice. So I didn't say anything.

I started walking toward the second hallway on the right and he followed. I looked at him out of the corner of my eye. He was staring at one of the preps at her locker. *Oh great,* I thought, *he's the type who hits on preps.* Then I noticed that his eyes had changed colors as he stared. They were black now. Ha, I knew he'd be a vampire, I was right!

But which side was he on, was he good or bad. I stopped; for he had stopped and he was still staring at the girl. I saw his teeth grow slightly. I grabbed his arm; he retracted his teeth and turned his eyes blue again. Then he turned and looked at me. I shook my head.

"Don't attack her," I whispered, "she's not worth it."

"You know?" he whispered back, "How did you know? Did you see?"

He seemed scared that I knew. Surely he thought I was going to tell.

"Don't worry," I said, "I won't tell. I'm one too."

"Prove it" he said.

So I did, I turned my eyes black and made my teeth elongate. He smiled. I think he was for the same reason I was: someone who understands. I retracted my teeth and turned my eyes back to their original color.

"Finally" said Ryan, "*finally* someone who knows and understands what I'm going through!"

"Same here," I said happily.

"Wait, are you good or bad?" Ryan asked skeptically. The question I was longing to ask since I saw his black eyes.

"Good," I answered. "What about you?"

"I'm good too" he said, "I just attack animals."

The warning bell rang. Five minutes until the tardy bell. I started walking and Ryan followed. If I was late on the first day, what would my mom do; ground me? But wait I had an excuse: Ryan.

But I still didn't want to be late. We started to run. We were almost there two minutes until the bell. We had just walked through the door as the bell rang. We barely made it. And there sat Karla, she motioned me over; she'd saved me a seat. She was talking to me again.

CHAPTER 2
Still Friends

I took my seat beside Karla, and Ryan sat by me. Right after I sat down Karla slid a note on to my desk. I opened and read it. It said to meet her in the bathroom. When I had closed it and nodded she raised her hand and the teacher let her go. Then it was my turn. I raised my hand.

"Yes, Ashlee?" the teacher answered.

"I forgot my notebook in my locker could I go get it?" I said. I'd never been an extremely good liar.

Ryan looked over at me, shook his head, and turned and smiled the other way. He knew I was lying. I knew because I had the same ability: reading peoples' minds, seeing the future, knowing if people are lying. Totally normal. Well, for me anyway.

"Hurry." the teacher answered.

I got up and walked out the door. I had to go to my locker now. But that could wait. Seeing Karla was more important, as long as she didn't have news reporters with her. But I doubted that.

I found her in the bathroom waiting, no one with her, that was a good sign. She seemed to be deep in thought, and not have noticed me enter until I moved to lean against the wall.

"I'm sorry I haven't spoken to you." she said looking up at me.

"Yeah, I understand. It must have been weird for you to find out like that." I said looking down. "Sorry."

"Weird isn't the word, scary is more like it. And don't be sorry it's not your fault."

"Why are you still friends with me, even if we did promise to be friends forever, but you'd have the risk of me attacking you. Aren't you afraid of me?" I said confused.

"I *am* a little afraid, but you *need* me." said Karla. "And friends don't leave other friends to deal with stuff on their own."

"Wow thanks, you're so awesome. I . . ." I started.

"Why didn't you tell me? Who all knows? Why are you a vampire anyway?"

All the questions I hoped she wouldn't ask, thrown in my face all at once. I had to tell her. I couldn't hide it, she knows me too well for that. But what if she tells, I would have to hide for the rest of my life. Not being able to be like a normal kid.

"Oh, don't even think about that, you know I won't tell anyone. You're my best friend." she rolled her eyes; I told you she knows me too well.

"I know. Well, I never told you because it would risk our friendship; see how long it took you to talk to me again. Only you know. And I'll tell you the answer the other question some other time. You're not ready for it yet."

She didn't know there were other vampires. I was going to tell her, just after she was used to me. I think it would be safe to tell her in a couple of months. Yeah, *months*.

"Why can't you tell me why you're a . . ." Karla started.

"Don't say it someone might hear. I thought I heard something. Or it might be like yesterday."

"What happened yesterday? You hear something that's not there? Please say that's it."

"No, I thought I heard someone, but it was across town."

"Huh? Is that possible? Is that *normal*?"

"Yeah, well for me it is anyway." I shrugged.

"Oh. Interesting. How?"

"Tell you later, we got to go."

We went back to class, not at the same time. I went first. When I walked in everyone looked, even the teacher, and he never looks.

"I couldn't find it." I lied as I took my seat.

"There can't be that much stuff in your locker." the teacher exclaimed.

Karla walked in as he spoke.

"Well, there's stuff in it from last year. I forgot to clean it, sorry I wasted time."

The teacher turned around and resumed writing on the board. Then Ryan slid me a note. I looked over at him, he was pretending to look out the window, but was looking at me out of the corner of his eye.

"I know you're looking." I whispered. He smiled.

I opened the note and read it. It had my name on it. How did he know my name? I read on, it said, 'you liar'. I wrote back, 'hey I don't deny it. And how do you know my name.'

I slid it back; he grabbed it as soon as I took my hand off of it. He opened it quickly, which kind of freaked me out. He leaned toward me.

"The teacher said it when he answered you." he said quietly.

CHAPTER 3

Scammed

The bell rang. Yes! This class was over. Everyone got up and ran to the door, as if that would help the day go by faster. Karla, Ryan, and I were the last out of the room. We walked together, but Ryan didn't seem to like Karla being with us, and Karla didn't even seem to notice Ryan. So I walked in the middle.

"Oh, yeah" I said. "I haven't introduced you two yet have I?" They didn't talk. They just kept looking in front of them.

"Anyway, Ryan," he looked over. "This is Karla." he nodded. "Karla, Ryan."

Karla showed no affection; just tossed a sideways glance of hatred at Ryan then smiled at me.

I was never so happy to see that we were almost to class. My two friends, at least I thought Ryan was my friend, that are in almost all my classes hate each other. Great.

I took my seat between Karla and Ryan. Then Ryan handed me a note. It said 'I don't like Karla' so I asked why, and then slid it back. He opened it then smiled. He looked at me.

"I don't trust her. I know she knows . . . and I know how." he whispered. "But just watch out, okay. She's having second thoughts and she wants to tell."

I just looked at him. I know how he knew; I just didn't know why he was so worried. Karla's my best friend.

"I know this is your best friend, but I'm serious. If you don't believe me look for yourself. You can read minds right?" said Ryan.

"Yeah, I can, but . . ."

"Then check. I swear I'm not lying."

"It's not . . . I just . . . I've never read *her* mind before."

"What?" Ryan said a little too loudly.

The teacher looked at him. He was smiling. Evidently he thought Ryan was asking about what he was saying.

"What's your name?" the teacher asked.

"Ryan, sir." Ryan said nervously, thinking he was in trouble.

"Well, thank you Ryan, for showing some interest in my class on the first day."

The teacher went off explaining to Ryan what he had just said. But Ryan didn't listen.

"Sorry about that." he said to me. "You haven't though?"

"No . . . I mean she is after all my best friend and I . . ." Ryan cut me off.

"Really need to know what she is thinking about doing to you. She was thinking of meeting you in the bathroom at lunch with . . ." he stopped and looked over at Karla. "With news reporters."

I felt my jaw drop. How could she do that? And who should I believe. It was just crazy. I looked over at her; she saw me and smiled getting out a piece of paper. I turned back to Ryan.

"You can't be serious. Please just tell me you're joking." I said, almost in tears.

"I'm sorry, but check for yourself." he said.

"I can't."

"Why can't you?"

"I just can't."

"You have to. Can you at least try?"

Karla passed me a note. I turned and looked at her, she smiled, I turned back to Ryan and opened the note. She said to meet her in the bathroom at lunch. Was Ryan right? He was right about the bathroom thing.

*   *   *

"Told you." said Ryan after he got done reading the note in our next class.

This was the only class we had that Karla didn't. Karla hated chemistry so she didn't take it. So now we could talk about her.

"Yeah, but that doesn't mean you were right about the reporters." I said.

"Read her mind then. Just do it, I don't care if she's your best friend."

"But . . ."

"Do it!"

"Fine, I will when I see her!"

I can't believe I had to invade my friend's privacy. I'd do it in our next class, because she was in that one. I really hoped Ryan read her mind wrong. If that was possible.

"Good, when's that?" said Ryan.

"Next class. Do I really have . . . ?"

"Yeah you really have to."

"Oh, alright."

So I really did have to. I hate my life.

*   *   *

"Hey, Karla, what's up?" I said when I saw her.

I needed something to distract her though. Great there was a big hole in the plan. The universe must love me!

"I'll distract her for you." Ryan said smiling.

And the universe hates me again. Wonderful.

"Thanks, Ryan. That'd be fantastic!" I said sarcastically.

"You're welcome."

He walked over to Karla and started talking. This was my only chance. I looked straight into the pupils of her eyes, and suddenly my mind was full of her thoughts. This was how I normally found out what I was getting for Christmas and birthdays. I pulled back to my own thoughts and Ryan noticed. He stopped in mid-sentence, turned, and walked over to me.

"So what did you realize? Your best friend is scamming you? That she doesn't really care?" he said as he sat down beside me.

"She *is* going to try to tell. Everyone." I said staring at Karla. "I can't believe it. It's like she's turning into a prep."

"Ashlee, your eyes." Ryan warned.

"Oh. Yeah . . . forgot . . . sorry."

"Why are you apologizing to me? It's not like you can help it."

"I know. Why would she do that?" I said angrily.

"I know you're mad. But some people are just like that. Mostly because they're afraid of us."

I knew he was right, but I just can't admit it to myself. I had to stop talking to Karla. This is just wonderful. Why did all of this have to happen to me?

"Hey, Ashlee" Karla whispered. "Your friend, Ryan, is really weird."

I turned and looked at Ryan he was looking straight ahead. He realized I was looking at him so he leaned over and whispered to me.

"I was telling her about the life cycle of bees." He said grinning.

Okay, I had to admit, it would be weird if someone randomly came up to you and started talking about *that*. That'd be slightly creepy.

"I'll write you a note." I told Ryan as the teacher walked in.

The teacher turned his back to the class and I passed the note. As soon as I straightened back up, Karla passed me a note. According to her there was another new kid. I slid the note into my book. Then Ryan handed his back to me.

I asked him why bees. He just put he didn't know. I leaned toward him.

"Random, much?" I said smiling.

"Just a little. Are you going to meet, 'that girl' in the bathroom?" he said.

"No, I'm not that stupid. There's a new kid."

"Now that was random. Girl, boy? Name?

"Girl, I think her name is Jafar."

"Where's she from?"

"I don't know. What do you think I am? A mind reader?" I laughed.

"Whatever." Ryan chuckled.

CHAPTER 4
Friend Issues

"You should sit with me at lunch." I told Ryan at our lockers, which happen to be right beside each other.

"Okay, to make sure Karla doesn't sit there?"

"No, because I want you to . . . duh! And I have a feeling Karla will be waiting in the bathroom all during lunch anyway."

"True." he said laughing. "When's that new kid coming?"

"Right about now." I said pointing at the door.

She was about five inches shorter than me. She had wavy blonde hair that came past her elbows, and really bright blue eyes. She's a prep, she had to be.

She walked straight to the prep tables and sat down. They didn't say anything. Yep, she was one of *them*.

"Great, like there needs to be more of them." I said.

"I know what you mean." Ryan said staring at her with hatred.

"You're talking about my eyes turning black, yours are way worse right now." I whispered so only he could hear.

"Oh, yeah. My bad." he said blinking.

After blinking five times his eyes were back to normal. But you could still tell he wanted to do away with her. I did too but I didn't show it *that* much.

I think the world would be better if there were no social statuses. Everyone: humans, vampires, werewolves, and people like that; would just get along. But that'll never happen. Preps think they're too good for that.

* * *

"Hey, Ashlee, why didn't you meet me at lunch?" Karla said as we sat down in our next class.

"I guess I was just hungry. You know, they actually had something half-way decent today." I said.

"No, I didn't know that, because I was waiting for you in the bathroom the whole time!"

"Sorry, just calm down. I bet it wasn't that important."

"Actually, it *was* that important. You've been hanging out with that new kid and totally ignoring me!"

"What do you want me to do about it?"

"Well, for one, stop hanging out with him! Duh!"

"You can just deal with it. I'm not picking between friends. If you don't like him, then don't be my friend anymore!" I was losing my temper: that was bad.

"You're going to have to pick!" Karla shouted.

"THAT'S IT. YOU'RE DEAD!" I had had it.

I couldn't tell if my eyes were black, but I jumped over the desk and punched her in the mouth regardless. Then I saw the blood taunting me. I was gazing at it when Ryan took me by the hand and dragged me out of the room.

In the hallway he made me sit down, then went to the door and looked through the window. He looked away immediately after, probably because the blood. He looked down at me.

"Nice going, you almost blew it." he said to me.

"What do you mean?" I asked.

"Well, your eyes turned black right before you jumped over the desk, and then when you saw the blood your teeth grew a little."

"I didn't mean to." I said, "You understand right?"

"Of course I do, that's why I pulled you out of there before everyone saw you."

"What's going on in there now?" I asked pointing at the door.

"Nothing really. Just everyone is crowding around her, that's all."

After this I was going to be dead because my mom would kill me. Ryan bent down and got the hair out of my face. Evidently my hair had fallen down when I jumped over the desk. He looked me in the eyes.

"You're in so much trouble, you know that?"

I didn't answer. I wasn't actually listening. I hadn't achieved my goal. I hadn't killed Karla, I didn't finish the job. I had to finish her off. I couldn't let it go now.

"Hey, are you listening?" Ryan said, making me come back to reality.

"No, I wasn't sorry. I was thinking." I said.

"I said you're going to be in a lot of trouble."

"Obviously."

"Yeah, that's why I said it."

"Hey I have a job to do. Could you help me with it?" I said half listening to him.

"That depends on what it is." he answered looking suspicious.

"Come down here."

He bent down.

"What?" he said.

"I have to kill Karla." I whispered in his ear.

"What, why?"

"Because she deserves it. And didn't you hear me?"

"Yeah, I heard you, you said: 'That's it. You're dead.' but louder."

"Yeah, and I meant it. I don't back down on my word." I said.

I was really mad. 'I have to kill her', I kept repeating in my head, 'I have to kill her.' But why?

"I understand, and I'll help you." Ryan said unexpectedly.

"Thanks, but I have to be the one to kill her."

"Alright, when are we doing this exactly?"

"Tonight, while she's asleep."

"Okay, I see one problem. I've not the slightest idea where she lives. I just moved here, remember?"

"Yeah, that's why you're going to meet me in the park. Do you know where that is?"

"Sure, okay. I'll find it." he got up and looked through the door. "We have to move now."

"Why?"

"Just come on."

He helped me up and we started walking down the hall. Once we turned the corner I heard a door shut. It had to be the classroom door. They were taking her to the nurse.

We walked to the second floor and walked around a few times. We just talked.

"If we do this, does it make us bad vampires?" I asked Ryan worriedly.

"No. You have a reason. If you don't kill her she'll tell everyone. Especially after punching her." he said.

"Okay and . . ."

"And you're not killing her for her blood. You're just killing her, quick and easy."

"Okay, so we're still good though?"

"Yeah, we're still good. Let's go back now. I think it's safe for you to go." he said looking at his watch.

We walked back down to the classroom and walked in. Everyone looked at me when I walked in behind Ryan. They all looked happy. One of the preps came up to me smiling.

"What, do you want some too?" I asked, not in the mood.

"No, no, no, just wanted to talk to you." she looked at Ryan and added, "Alone."

"Don't worry. I'm gone." he said, he winked at me, he could hear from long distances.

He walked away and sat in a vacant desk at the back of the room farthest away from the door where no one else was sitting around him.

"So, anyway, loved the way you took care of the nobody." she said.

"I'm a nobody too. Who are you?" I said flatly.

"I'm Nicole, and now it's your choice about that 'nobody' thing. Do you want to sit with us at lunch tomorrow?"

"I couldn't if I wanted to; I'm going to be suspended."

"The teacher said she won't tell the principal that you did that, she's going to say that Karla fell."

"Well, my answer is going to be the same either way."

"What's your answer?"

"No."

"What? Why would you say *no*?"

"Because, I don't want to be a stuck-up, snotty little, preppy girl. Kind of like what you are." I said and walked away.

I walked over and sat down beside Ryan. He looked at me like he thought I was stupid. He shrugged his shoulders at me.

"Why didn't you go with that? You could've been popular." he said.

"Well, I've already got where I want to be." I said smiling.

"You're so stupid. You know that?"

"You might think that now, but if I said yes to her you'd be sitting alone at lunch." I teased, "think about that."

"Good point."

The teacher came back in the classroom and walked straight up to the board and started writing the lesson. I really wasn't getting in trouble. Ryan nudged me. I smacked his hand away. He tried again, and this time I jumped up. He touched my most ticklish spot: my ribs. I sat down quickly and looked at him.

"What? I'm trying to work." I said, barely moving my lips and clenching my teeth to stop myself from laughing.

"I need to talk to you at our lockers, so hang back. Okay?" he said.

"Yeah. Sure. Whatever."

Why did I want to kill Karla? I don't even know. Probably half of it was because she wanted to tell everyone that I'm a vampire, and half because she was trying to make me pick between my friends.

CHAPTER 5
The Kill

A t the end of the day I waited at the lockers like Ryan asked. But I don't know why when his locker was right under mine. When he got done he made a motion with his hand that we should go. But he didn't say anything until we were outside.

"Do you walk home or ride the bus?" he asked.

"I walk home. Why?" I said.

"Just wondering. Is it alright if I go to your house?"

"Should be. Why?"

"My mom is still moving all our stuff into the new house, she said if I make a friend and they said I could come over I had her permission."

"Oh, yeah my mom probably won't care."

"Thanks. And it makes it easier for us to go to Karla's house too."

"Yeah, and you're walking the wrong way. My house is this way." I said pointing.

"Right, I knew that. I was just seeing if you knew." Ryan said slightly embarrassed.

"It's my house, how could I not know that?"

"Sometimes, sarcasm hurts." he joked.

We walked the five blocks to my house. It was a very quiet walk. I realized he didn't talk as much as I had thought. When we got there I had him stop at the door to give him a warning.

"Okay, just so you know my parents and brother have no idea I'm a vampire, and I want to keep it that way. And my parents may ask you a lot of questions, my brother will ignore you, and that's sometimes a good thing. And my parents will say something totally embarrassing. Then we can go up to my room." when he looked confused I added, "did you get all that?"

"Yeah, sure." he said, "something about your parents and brother and stuff."

I rolled my eyes and opened the door. As I had suspected my mom came running in and attacked me with a hug.

"Too . . . much . . . hugging!" I said, being suffocated.

"Sorry." she said letting go, "Ashlee who's this complete stranger and why's he in our house?"

"Don't worry she calls everyone a stranger." I told Ryan, "even if she does know them."

Ryan nodded.

"I'm Ryan Ma'am." he said and he shook my mom's hand. At that moment my dad walked in, "and you must be Ashlee's dad, I'm Ryan." and he shook my dad's hand too.

"Yeah, we were just going to go up to my room and do some extra credit." I said taking Ryan's hand and starting for the stairs.

"What's your hurry?" my dad said, "We want to talk to your new friend."

"Fine, do you want anything to drink or eat Ryan?" I said.

"No. Thank you though." my brother walked in as he spoke.

"Hey kiddo. How was school?" I asked him messing up his hair.

He hugged me, then looked at Ryan and answered.

"It was great we got candy in every class. One of the kids threw up and it was all . . ." he started.

"Okay, we don't really want to know what it looked like little one." I stopped him.

"Fine then, I won't tell you how it was all chunky and green." he said quickly.

"Ew, how's that great?"

"We got candy . . . duh!"

"Oh, yeah that changes *everything*. Ryan this is my little brother, Adam, but he goes by Duke." I told Ryan.

"Hi. Just so you know my sister's a nerd, she loves extra credit and stuff." Duke said shaking hands with Ryan.

"Why does everyone in this family shake hands with people?" I said, "Hey, Duke, could you go turn my computer on?"

"Yeah," he answered. Then mumbled, "nerd."

"I heard that." I turned to my parents. "Can we go upstairs now, please?"

"I guess." my mom said before my dad could speak.

Ryan and I went up to my room; Duke was still turning the computer on. He turned when we entered. On the screen was the start up password.

"I need the password." Duke said, "and if you was coming up here anyway, why'd you have me turn this on?"

"Because I thought mom would talk forever." I said.

"Okay. I need your password though."

"Like I'm going to give you my password. Move over."

He moved and I typed in my password. The screen flashed the welcome message then went to my home page. My brother looked up at me.

"You want me to leave now?" he asked.

"Yes, please." I looked over my shoulder at Ryan as Duke left. "Come over here."

He walked over as I was getting online. Then I typed in 'vampires'. Five pages of results came up, one of which said 'Evil Vampires Names and Felonies.' I clicked on it.

"What exactly are you doing?" Ryan said.

"I'm showing you the person who turned me into what I am." I said scrolling down.

"Oh, they have that stuff on the internet?"

"Yeah. The password I put in when the computer was starting up makes it possible for me to see this stuff."

"So it's like a secret computer network for people like us. Why don't I know then?"

"Well, I just found out yesterday. There was an email from some girl that I didn't know; it had the password in it."

"Okay then?"

"Here he is! Right there, Alexander. Read that right there, it says why he's on here."

"I know what it says, because that's the same man who turned me into a . . . ," he looked at the door and whispered, "a vampire."

"You can say it louder; my brother doesn't listen to my conversations."

"Oh, okay. But, when did Alexander turn you into a vampire?"

"May 25, 1999 at 2:15pm. Why?"

"That's the same month, day, and year he attacked me, but he attacked me ten minutes after you. Weird."

"Yeah. Are you staying for dinner?"

"Random but sure."

"Hey, dinner's ready, get down here." my mom's voice sounded from down stairs.

We ran down stairs and went to the dining room. My brother was setting the table, my dad was pouring the drinks, and my mom was putting the food on the table. Ryan and I slipped into seats. After dinner had been going on for a while, my dad and Ryan started a conversation about economics. Boring.

"My mom was getting gas the other day and started complaining about the price being too high." Ryan said.

"Oh, well we don't have to worry about prices." my dad said.

"Oh really? Why?"

"Hey, who wants pie?" I said shaking my head at my dad.

"Mom didn't make pie." said Duke.

"Thanks for playing along, Adam."

"You haven't told your new friend, have you?" my dad said, choking on his water.

"No. I know you told me to tell so that I wouldn't be lying, but . . ."

"Tell him. I won't tell for you this time."

"But . . ."

"Do it."

"Fine. Ryan, I'm rich. I don't normally tell people because they'll end up liking me for my stuff."

He just stared at me. Probably thinking I was crazy for not telling anyone and becoming popular. But I didn't care about that, I wanted to know if he would turn on me like all my other 'friends'.

"Oh, that's it? I thought it was bad." he said relived.

"See? Not everyone is like your old friends." my dad told me.

"Ryan, could you come with me? I need to talk to you." I said to Ryan.

I got up and he followed me back upstairs to my room. I opened the door and let him in first then I walked in and shut the door.

"Why didn't you tell me?" Ryan said right after the door had shut.

"I already told you the reason down stairs. Anyway there's something more important right now. Look at the time." I said.

"Oh, I see what you mean. Should we go now?"

"Yeah, but not that way." he was at the door. "Window."

"Why?"

"Wouldn't it be weird if I was to go down stairs and tell my mom 'hey we're going to Karla's house in the middle of the night to kill her,' that'd be really normal, wouldn't it?"

"Okay, but how?"

"I have my ways. Look out the window."

He moved over to the window, and looked out and down. There was a ladder tilted to the window.

"You're so smart, you know that?"

"Yeah, just go down the ladder."

He went down. I forgot to warn him the last six steps were missing but I knew it was too late when I heard him slip, then a thud.

"Could've warned me." he said.

"Sorry, I forgot."

I went down and at the last step I froze. The stool I normally used to get down the rest of the way was gone.

"Darn it. My dad must've moved it." I whispered to myself.

"Moved what?"

"The stool that used to be right there." I said pointing.

"That's how you get out."

"Yeah."

"Here, I'll help you."

He grabbed me around the waist and I let go of the ladder. I was in the air for a second then I felt ground. I turned around to face Ryan.

"Thanks." I said. "let's go."

We walked across the yard to the gate. I held the gate open for him then walked out and made sure the door didn't slam.

"Which way now?" Ryan said.

"That way. Across the street three houses down."

We walked in the shadows over to Karla's house, then we walked around the house to the back gate and went into the back yard. There was normally a ladder at her window, and there it sat.

"Yes. It's here." I said moving to the ladder.

"Why do you both have a ladder at your window?"

"We made an agreement when we were friends. Could you help me up? She's missing steps too."

"Here, stand right there." he pointed in the darkness.

He picked me up and sat me down on the first step. I looked over my shoulder at him. He was getting ready to come up.

"Do you need my help?" I said.

"No. I got it." he said, and he jumped up.

I climbed on up. There was a platform at the top. I climbed onto it and got out of Ryan's way.

"You have to go in first." I said as Ryan got up.

"Ashlee, why can't you?"

"Because you have to hold her mouth shut so no one hears her scream."

"Whatever." he rolled his eyes.

I opened the window and he stepped in quietly. I stepped in after him, walked over to the door and shut it as Ryan moved over to the bed side and looked down at Karla. I gave him the signal and he quickly and quietly moved one hand on her mouth and the other behind her head. Her eyes opened immediately. She looked up and found me right in her face.

Her eyes were wide with horror, but I ignored that. I looked at Ryan and he nodded. I moved my face quickly to her neck and sunk my teeth into a tender spot. The blood was filling; I'd never had that much blood at once. I could hear her muffled screams in Ryan's hand. Her face was getting pale and her screams becoming faint.

Then, all of a sudden they stopped. And she lay motionless on her bed. Ryan put his hand on her chest.

"She's dead now." he said, and I pulled away.

"Are you sure?" I said, blood dripping from my mouth.

"Yes, go open the door and let's get out of here. What's the matter? Are you okay?" he looked at me, I was crying.

"Yeah, I'm fine." I said wiping my eyes.

"Come on let's go."

He grabbed my hand and took me to the window. He went out first so he could help me when I went down. I took one last look at Karla's corpse before the windowsill blocked my view. Ryan was waiting at the bottom of the ladder.

After he helped me down I immediately started walking. He ran to catch up with me. But he didn't say anything. He kept looking at me out of the corner of his eye. I could tell he was suspicious of me, thinking I was acting funny: different than usual.

"Are you sure you're okay?" he said, looking directly at me now.

"Huh . . . oh, yeah, I'm fine." I was only half listening to what he was saying.

He didn't take his eyes off of me after that. He didn't even watch where he was walking, yet he didn't run into or trip over anything. It was like he knew everything was there and exactly where it was. Duh . . . he's a vampire, we have that ability. Killing Karla was messing with my mind.

"What time is it?" Ryan asked suddenly.

"Huh . . . what?" I wasn't listening.

"What time is it?" he repeated.

"Oh, I don't know probably around midnight."

"I'd better go home then. Do you want me to walk you home first?"

"It doesn't matter."

"You have something on your mind. What is it?"

"Nothing to worry about."

We kept walking and Ryan was still suspicious that something was bothering me. Problem was, he was right, something was bothering me. I had just killed my best friend. It was like a nightmare I'd never wake up from. Her muffled screams were still ringing in my ears. What had I done?

"Ashlee?" Ryan turned and looked at me.

I had stopped. The guilt made me stop. Soon the guilt would kill me from the inside out. It'd kill me emotionally first then finish me off physically.

"Ashlee, are you sure you don't want to talk about it?"

"I . . . I just killed . . . my best friend. I hate myself for this." I was talking more to myself but Ryan talking back made me feel better.

"You can't hate yourself. You had to do it, if you didn't everyone would know your secret. But you will have second thoughts, you'll have regrets, and the guilt will tear you up emotionally. I've already been there."

"What do you mean you've 'already been there'?"

"Two years after I was turned into a vampire I attacked my best friend. I couldn't help it though. The thirst for blood was too strong but now I know how to avoid it."

"Well, maybe keeping my secret is less important."

CHAPTER 6
The Guilt

"Ashlee, honey, wake up. I've got some bad news." my mom said, waking me up three hours later.

"W . . . what is it? Is everything alright mom?" I said, rubbing my eyes.

"No, everything's not alright. Your friend, Karla, she was killed last night. They think it was by some type of animal, there were teeth marks on her neck. Very unusual teeth marks."

"What? Are you serious?"

"I'm so sorry honey. You stay in bed. You don't have to go to school."

"Okay, thanks mom."

"I'll leave you alone now."

She got up and walked out the door. I momentarily saw my dad when the door opened. I got up after it had shut and listened to what they were saying.

"How'd she take it?" I heard my dad ask.

"She's so devastated, she doesn't believe that Karla's really gone." my mom answered.

I walked back to my bed. I couldn't listen anymore. What would happen if they found out it was me? But that was impossible. The teeth marks could only be traced to me if they knew what my teeth marks looked like when I had the fangs.

"I'm going to work and so is your dad. We're going to take your brother to school too." my mom said a while later as I came down stairs for breakfast.

"Okay. Bye mom, dad, Duke. I'll see you guys later." I said as they walked out the door.

"Bye honey. Be good."

After they were gone I went back upstairs and got back in bed. Several minutes later there was a tap at my window. Thinking it was just a tree or something, I turned on my side. Then there was a few more taps, too hard to have been a tree. I slowly turned over to face the window. There, standing on the ladder, was

Ryan. He didn't look like he had before. He was sad; all dressed in black and looking at me mournfully. I got up and let him in, then I went straight back to my bed.

"What?" I asked, frowning into my pillow.

"I just wanted to see if you were okay. I was worried you'd try to do something stupid." he blushed. I blushed at his concern.

"Oh. Well I'm fine. I haven't done anything stupid . . . yet."

"Don't say that. I know you won't do anything stupid, ever." he paused. "And that's why I'm here, well half of the reason. I'm here to make sure you don't do anything rash."

"I wasn't planning to. I was planning on staying here all day so I don't have to hear about what I've done. Everyone at school knows by now, they'd had to have figured out that she's . . . dead." my voice faded as I said the word. "What's the other half of your reason?"

He looked at me confused.

"For being here." I said.

"Oh, that. Um . . . well, I don't know really, I just wanted to see you because I knew you wouldn't be at school."

I just looked at him. How did he know? Could he see the future, like I could? Though I always resist the temptation.

"I can't see the future, but I do know it would lead to suspicion if you *did* show up."

"How so?" I looked at him confused.

"Well, you were her best friend. It would be . . . abnormal . . . for anyone to go to school after . . ." he cut off.

"Yeah. I suppose it would."

He walked over and sat on my bed. I sat up to see his face. He looked like he was concentrating on something that I couldn't see. He looked at me, expression changing to concern, and put his arm around my shoulders. I looked at him carefully then put my arms around his waist.

"Do you want to know how desperate I am not to believe she's gone? And that I'm the cause of it?" I said, breaking the silence.

He looked at me with curious eyes.

"When I woke up this morning," I continued. "I was hoping it was just a dream, well, nightmare actually. But the hope was obviously wasted. Wasted on the most stupid purpose. I shouldn't care, should I? Because she was going to tell everyone. But I can't help feeling so guilty." I looked him straight in the eyes. "Is that bad?"

"She *was* your best friend Ashlee." he whispered. "It's not bad, it's just natural."

"Okay."

Then, at the exact moment I spoke, I remembered what my mom had said. About the 'very unusual teeth marks.' There was bound to be a lot of investigators looking at *her* corpse. Highly skilled investigators.

"Ryan, do you have the ability to see into the past? Before we were born?" I asked in an urgent tone.

"Yeah. Why?"

"Has there ever been a time when humans knew we existed?"

"Hold on a sec." he shut his eyes tightly for a few seconds that felt more like hours.

"Yes, there has." he reported.

"About how many years ago?"

"Twenty-five at the least." he paused. "Exactly twenty-five."

"Oh crap! Do you know what this means? There's a bunch of investigators looking at that corpse! How old do you think they'd be? Well, I think they'd be about thirty years old. *Thirty*! What does that mean? Do you know what that means?" I was shouting.

He looked at my terrified face for a few seconds then realization flashed onto his face.

"Oh," he choked out the word.

"You see the problem." I stated, and he nodded in agreement.

* * *

"Ashlee, we're home. Come down here." my mom yelled up the stairs.

Ryan had left to go to school so people wouldn't be suspicious. As soon as he left I cried myself to sleep. I'd woken up just seconds before my family had come in. I might as well not keep her waiting.

I slowly got up from my bed. I could feel that my hair was sticking in every direction and that it was tangled with tears. I didn't care. As I went down the stairs, not paying attention, I ran into something and fell backwards. I looked up and it was Ryan.

"Are you okay?" he said, helping me up. "I'm sorry."

"I'm perfectly all right." I sighed.

I walked around him and went into the kitchen. He followed me. My mom was waiting there. She took in my appearance then laughed.

"You look horrible." she chuckled.

"That much I know." I said flatly. She stopped laughing.

"Are you all right?" she said, alarmed by my voice.

"Perfectly so. Do you have my work that I missed?"

"That's why I'm here. I have your work and I'm supposed to explain it to you." Ryan answered.

"Thanks," my voice was so dead that I barely recognized it.

"Let's go up to your room and get started on it."

"Whatever."

I turned and ran back up the stairs. Out of the corner of my eye I saw Ryan and my mom share a worried glance, and then Ryan ran after me. I went right into my room, waited for him to come in then slammed the door. He jumped.

I ignored him and jumped into my bed pulling the covers over my face. I felt him sit down. Then he yanked the covers back. He was staring at me with a worried expression. I glared at him.

"What?" I asked.

"What's wrong?"

"You already know what's wrong." I said then turned over.

"Yes, but that's not the only thing bothering you. I can tell. Do you want to talk about it?"

"Well, you know how there's people looking at the puncture marks?" I asked, after all he was the only one I could talk to about this.

"Yes."

"And how they may figure out it's from a vampire?"

"Yes.

"Well, what happens if they do?"

"Well, they'll probably make a list of people she was friends with, then people she didn't like. Then they'll probably interrogate them." he paused. "We will most likely be on the top of that list."

"What do we do when that happens?"

"You mean *if* that happens. And I don't think it will. You have to remember they were only five at the time."

"But that's not something you forget now is it?"

"It's nothing to worry about. They probably *did* forget."

I turned over to face him. "Do you want me to prove that it will happen? Because I can if you want."

"Fine. How?" he mumbled.

"I can see the future . . . remember?" I rolled my eyes at him.

I closed my eyes and the vision came. It was of many posters littering the walls lining a street. The posters said the names of people needed for questioning. My name was the first on the list, Ryan's was second. Then Ryan and I, holding hands, passed through the scene, followed by a crowd of people. A mob.

I heard Ryan gasp and opened my eyes. His face was terrorized. He'd been reading my mind.

"Told you." I whispered.

"Ashlee," he said, barely audible. "You do know why there was a crowd behind us?"

"Yes. The mob was running us out of town."

"And I'm guessing you know why."

"Most likely because I blabbed."

He nodded. "You have to be careful what you tell them. Promise me, Ashlee?"

"I'll try." I sighed.

I sat up and Ryan laughed under his breath. He started poking at my hair.

"Is my hair really that bad?" I asked.

"No, no. You look fine." he stopped laughing as I got up. "Where are you going? I'm sorry if I hurt your feelings."

"No, you didn't." I sat at my computer and turned it on.

"What're you doing?"

He walked over and stood over me.

"Checking the vamp news bulletins."

I typed in the startup password and waited. I got on the internet as soon as it was done loading and typed in 'vampire world: news' then had to wait again. I was beginning to get impatient. Then it popped up. I read through it quickly:

VAMPIRE TRAGEDY

There has been the killing of a young, human girl. This killing is possible to expose us like the last time in 1984. And like last time we will execute the vampire(s) responsible.

In 1984 one of us had killed 108 humans in a month (which is impossible for a mere human) and did not dispose of the evidence. Investigators then studied the marks in the humans' necks. They had not considered vampires until the vampire responsible returned to the last human he fed off of. The humans saw the teeth and reported it to the people.

Their people lived in terror while our kind was forced into hiding. It took three years for the commotion to die down. After which we could start blending in again.

Ryan and I gasped at the same time. I looked up at him, and he bent down to level with me. He quickly kissed me on the cheek.

"I hope you're a really good actress." he said.

"Yeah. I am." I said dazed.

He laughed at whatever expression and pulled me against his chest. He kissed my forehead.

"I hope *you* are a good actor" I mumbled against his chest.

This made him laugh again.

"Of course I am." he chuckled.

I sighed and pushed my face deeper into his chest.

"What's bothering you now?"

"What should we do? Should we run?"

"No, we can't run. That would be much too conspicuous. We have to stay here, when we get called in for questioning we lie our way out of it. If that's possible for you, seeing as you might tell." he pulled me back to look me in the eyes and then he winked. "I know you won't tell."

"Yeah. At least one of us thinks so." I smiled.

He started laughing. I realized then that I'd never paid much attention to what Ryan looked like. Like the fact that he has dimples. Cute freckles scattered across his nose. Pretty blue eyes; I had trouble looking away from them, and the most beautiful smile I'd ever seen. Then realization hit again: I realized that I was in love with him.

CHAPTER 7

Love and Conspiracy

I opened my eyes staring at my bedroom door. I didn't remember Ryan ever leaving. He probably left after I fell asleep. All I remembered was him crawling back through my window after pretending to leave.

I closed my eyes and turned over. As I did so I hit something. That something said *ow*. My eyes flew open and I sat up as fast as I could. It was early in the morning. Probably not even after three. Still dark outside. I looked down beside me to find Ryan smiling up at me.

I fell back on the pillows and scooted closer. He was so warm. I hadn't realized I was cold until then. I kept inching closer until there was no space left between us.

Ryan, slightly confused, freed his arm and wrapped it around my shoulders. He shivered slightly as I nestled my face in his chest. He wasn't confused anymore.

He thought that I wanted to get warm. But I just wanted his arms around me. I smiled at my slyness.

"Hello." he said.

"Hi." I chuckled. "What are you here for?"

"Oh, I can leave if you want."

I grabbed his shirt as he started to pull away.

"No. Stay. Please?"

He laughed quietly at my child-like behavior. He had a beautiful laugh to match his beautiful smile.

"How long have you been here?" I asked.

"All night." he said after he stopped laughing.

"Wow. Why?"

"Well, I didn't really want to leave."

I blushed. He was probably blushing too, but I couldn't see his face and I didn't want to move to try.

"Oh." was all I could say.

"Yeah, um so what are you doing today?" he asked hesitantly.

"I don't know. Why?"

"Well, I was thinking, if you're not doing anything that is, if you wanted to um . . ."

"What is it you were thinking? Just tell me."

"Well, do you want to go somewhere today? With me?"

"Sure. I'd love to!" I would go anywhere with him.

"Really? With me? Just me and you? Alone?"

"Yeah, that'd be great!"

"Seriously? You're not just setting me up, are you?"

"Why would I set you up?" I asked confused.

"Well, I've never actually went out with anyone before. I have no experience. You probably have a lot of it." he mumbled.

"What? What do you mean that I probably have a lot of it?"

"Well, someone as beautiful as you is bound to have had a million boyfriends already."

I picked up my head and looked at his face. He was frowning. I lifted my hand to his mouth and pushed the corner of it up. He gently pushed my hand away, so I wrapped my arm around his neck and slid up face to face with him on the pillow. His eyes were closed, but when I kissed him for half a second straight on the lips his eyes flew open.

"I've never had a boyfriend." I whispered.

"This town is full of idiots then." he said.

I laughed. When I stopped he pulled my face closer, our noses touching. He was staring into my eyes.

"That makes me feel loads better. You never having a boyfriend." he breathed, he turned his head slightly away and closed his eyes.

I moved his face back in front of mine and kissed him full on the lips again, longer this time. He opened his eyes after two seconds, but I didn't stop because they fluttered closed again. He didn't even put up a fight when I forced his mouth open, but after that he did start kissing back. It lasted a minute but we could have gone longer. The sound of my brother getting up broke us apart.

Our breathing was heavy; it took a second until I was able to talk. But Ryan spoke before I could.

"I think. Maybe. I should. Leave." he gasped.

"No, please don't leave! Hide under the bed." I whispered.

He smiled and kissed me on the cheek. Then rolled over off the bed and disappeared. My brother walked in a second later. My breathing was back to normal.

"Hey. Did I wake you up, sis?" Duke said when he noticed I was up. "I'm sorry; it sounded like someone was suffocating you."

I heard a giggle from under the bed, too quiet for Duke to hear but meant for me to hear.

"Oh, did it?" I said innocently.

"Yeah. When did you wake up?"

"Half a second before you came in." I lied.

"Alright. Are you okay?"

"More than okay, actually."

I heard another laugh.

"Okay. Wake me up in time for breakfast, okay?"

"Okay kid."

"Thanks." he said then turned and left the room shutting the door behind him.

Ryan crawled out from under the bed and lay back down beside me. This time he was sliding closer to me. He put his arms around my waist and pulled me closer. No distance between us. I sighed. I could stay here forever. Maybe I would.

It felt like ten seconds passed then my mom yelled for me. I sighed.

"I'll go out the window and come back through the door." Ryan breathed in my ear.

"Okay." I sighed again.

He laughed while he walked to my window. He turned to smile at me then crawled out onto the ladder. I ran over to my mirror, brushed my hair and put it in a ponytail. Then I ran to my closet, put on my favorite skinny jeans and my favorite black button-up shirt and kicked on my favorite shoes. After that I ran downstairs.

"Well you look nice." my mother commented.

"Thanks. Hey, is it alright if Ryan comes over for breakfast?" I said.

"Sure. You seem to like him."

"Yeah, he's a good friend."

"I meant more than that." she whispered.

"Oh. Well, kind of."

"I knew it! Well I definitely approve!"

"Thanks mom." at that second the doorbell rang.

I ran to get it before anyone else could. I opened it slowly and peeked through it. It was Ryan, and he too had changed into nicer clothes and took a comb through his hair. I stood aside to let him in. He poked me in the side as he passed.

"Hey." he said.

"Hi." I smiled.

"Hello, Ryan. Lovely to see you again. You look nice today." my mom said entering the conversation.

"Nice to see you, too. And thank you."

"Oh. Darn it. I was supposed to wake Duke up. I'll be right back." I said and ran upstairs.

I ran down to the end of the hall and opened Duke's door quietly. I walked over to the side of his bed.

"Aw, he looks so cute when his asleep," I whispered. "Duke wake up!" I yelled beside his ear.

His eyes flew open and he jerked around trying to get out of the sheets then fell off the other side of his bed.

"Breakfast is ready." I said softly.

"Thanks." he growled.

I turned and ran back down stairs. Ryan and my mom had gone into the kitchen. When I walked in they turned and looked at me. Ryan got up from his seat at the table, and my mom laughed. Ryan look a bit embarrassed so he sat back down. I smiled at him and walked over to my mom.

"Do you need any help?" I asked her.

"No, but thanks." she smiled.

I turned to walk away but she grabbed my arm and pulled me toward her.

"That boy is in love with you." she whispered so she thought only I would hear.

One glance at Ryan proved her wrong.

He was staring out the window and blushing.

"Mom!" I whispered, also blushing.

"I'm sorry. Go sit down." she chuckled.

I walked over and sat by Ryan. He looked at me with an odd expression in his eyes. I looked away as my mom sat food on the table; eggs, bacon, toast, pancakes, waffles, milk, coffee, tea, and orange juice.

One thing about my mom: she likes cooking.

"So what are you two doing on this lovely day?" mom asked making implications.

I glanced at Ryan. He was still blushing but now staring at me. He shrugged at me.

"I don't know. Walk around town maybe. Show Ryan around." I answered finally.

"That's very nice of you Ashlee." my mom commented.

"Yeah, I know."

"Shall we go now?" Ryan asked.

"Of course!" I grabbed his hand and ran to the door.

I called a farewell over my shoulder to my mother then walked quickly out the door.

Ryan and I walked all the way up the street and turned up a side street that led to the park. Ryan had no idea where we were going but he followed anyway.

"Where are we going?" he finally asked.

"The park." I said and pointed at the gates.

"Oh. It is a good day to go to the park. But you are supposed to be sad because . . . ."

"I know," I cut him off frowning. "I don't really want to think about it though."

"I'm sorry."

I sighed.

We were at the gates now. I led the way to my favorite tree in the park. I dropped Ryan's hand and climbed up to the third branch where I was completely hidden by leaves. He followed right behind me.

"What's up?" Ryan asked.

"Nothing, I'm just thinking about Karla." I sighed.

"I really am sorry about that."

"It's okay. I'll live."

He took my hand and put it on his face. I looked up at him. He was looking the opposite way watching a squirrel on the end of the limb. The squirrel froze, looked over at Ryan, and then jumped to the ground.

Ryan looked at me again. He noticed I was watching him and he smiled. I smiled back and looked away.

At that second someone walked up to the tree and sat at the base of it. With what I saw it looked like someone my age. And it was obviously a girl. She had waist length wavy blonde hair. I was immediately reminded of the new prep.

I crawled down a branch and leaned out over her. As I had thought, it was that Jafar girl. The only difference in her appearance was her eyes. Last time I'd seen them they were blue now they were purple.

I wondered what Little Miss. Prep would be doing in the park when she could be at the mall with all the guys. Maybe she had a secret prep meeting here or something. Hah!

A man walked up to her. I crawled back up to where Ryan was still sitting and listened. The guy looked a little familiar but I didn't know why. The prep stood up. Apparently this was who she was waiting for.

"Hello, Alexander." Jafar greeted him.

Ryan put his hand over my mouth because he knew I was going to hiss. I looked up at him and he shook his head at me. I nodded in agreement to his unspoken request: don't show them we were up here.

"Hello, my dear one. What do you have for me today?" Alexander said.

"That girl was not killed by an animal."

"I had already guessed at that. Anything else? Like do you know who it was?"

"No, not yet. But I will soon. I have two main suspects."

Ryan and I looked each other then back down at the two people below us.

"Who are they?"

"Two other vampires. Ashlee and Ryan. I do not know their last names."

"Look into it and find out what's going on with them. You have made me very hopeful today. Now go my little spy."

"Alex? Why does it matter who killed the girl?"

"Because we are going to ask them to join us."

"Aren't you still in hiding from creating all those vamps that got destroyed?"

"Yes. But they can still work for me." Alexander whispered, "Well I'll be on my way. It would be best if you don't hesitate to leave."

"Okay."

Alexander walked away at a very brisk pace and Jafar waited a few seconds then ran the opposite way.

I slowly climbed down the tree to the last branch. They were definitely gone. I continued to jump out of the tree. Ryan jumped out right after me.

I looked around the park. Nobody had noticed the little conversation held over here.

Ryan grabbed my hand. I leaned into his chest. He knew just as well as I did that those people were vampires and who they were. He was worried. So was I. Karla was a really big bloodstain on my life.

CHAPTER 8
The Change

It was November. All the leaves on the trees were multitudes of yellow and orange. It made the trees look as if they were on fire.

Jafar found Ryan and my last names. She hasn't told Alexander yet. That we know of at least. If she had we would have heard from someone asking us to join them. When they do we will say no, and that always leads to a fight.

Jafar found out everything about Ryan and me. She broke into the school's filing room and made copies of our records. She hasn't met up with Alexander. We've been keeping tabs on her, if she did anything else we would have noticed.

Right now Ryan was sitting outside of her house. Though Ryan and I were a couple now, we didn't go on dates much. Ever since we saw Alexander and Jafar were in cahoots with each other, we've been so involved with spying on Jafar. Not much alone time.

"Ashlee! Come down here!" my mom yelled.

I got up off my bed, walked out the door and went straight down the stairs. It was an instinctional thing. My mom was in the kitchen, as usual.

She was holding a folded piece of paper with my name on it. She was staring at it but looked up when I entered. She smiled at me and handed me the paper.

"Ryan." she told me as I took the note.

She, as well as I did, knew Ryan's hand writing. It wasn't hard to recognize. Especially after writing notes with him for a few months.

"Thanks mom." I smiled.

I ran back up stairs and nearly shut my leg in the door. As soon as I sat on my bed I unfolded the note and started reading:

Ashlee,
    Meet me at the tree. You know, "our" tree. I'll be waiting there at 6:15. I miss spending time with you. And I really want to see you again.
                                    - Ryan

P.S.

Jafar is going to the park. I believe her to be meeting Alexander.

That was the end of the note. So Jafar was going to the park. There's only one reason Miss. Princess would be going to the park; to meet Alexander. That was what we'd been waiting for. Why we'd been spying on her.

I slowly got up and walked over to my mirror. I brushed through my hair. Then I glanced over all the make-up my mother bought me that I never used and then at my pale, dead, and sick looking smiling face. Ryan said I was beautiful without make-up.

I turned, walked out my door, ran down the stairs, and walked straight into the kitchen. My mom was still in there, of course. Again, she looked up at my entrance.

"You meeting Ryan somewhere?" she asked.

"Yeah, what time is it?" I said.

"Six o'clock."

"Okay. Bye mom. I'm supposed to meet him at 6:15."

I ran out the door and ran all the way to "our" tree. Ryan was standing there waiting. When he saw me he smiled. I ran into his open arms. We stood that way for a while.

"I've missed you." he said.

"I've missed you too." I said, "But I just saw you right before we left school."

"I know, I just . . . . It's hard."

Why doesn't he just say he loves me already!?

"Yeah." I sighed.

We stopped hugging and looked toward the gates at the same time. Jafar was walking through them. I turned back to Ryan but he wasn't there. Then there was pressure on the tops of my arms as I was pulled up into the tree.

"Sorry," Ryan apologized. "Did I hurt you?"

"No. I'm fine." I said, and then looked down at the base of the tree.

Jafar was now standing there waiting. I looked up in time to catch a man walking through the gates; Alexander. My eyes followed him until he was at the bottom of the tree.

"Hello, Jafar. I'm sorry our meeting has been delayed for so long" Alexander said as he walked up.

"It's no problem, Alex. Here's all the information about Ashlee Teaford and Ryan Whiting you could possibly need." Jafar gushed happily as she handed him two folders.

"Teaford? Whiting? They are still alive?"

"What do you mean? Of course they are alive."

"I created them years ago. I didn't think they survived. And I surely never had the thought they would be friends."

"They're actually more than that." Jafar mumbled.

"Excuse me?"

"They are not just friends, they are a couple."

"Well, they'll love to join us, seeing as I'm their creator. They've probably sucked the life out of their families and have nothing left."

"On the contrary their families live. The only human they have ever killed is the girl. They don't feed the way we do."

Ryan wrapped his arms around my waist and put his chin on my shoulder.

"They haven't killed their families?" Alexander whispered shocked. "Well, we shall not judge them by their dietary habits. They would not judge ours."

"They *would* judge ours. They don't like vampires like us. They would never join us either."

"We shall see." Alexander grinned. "Good-bye child. Thank you for these files. I shall leave you now."

"Bye, Alex!" Jafar smiled.

They both left. Ryan put me on his back and jumped out of the tree. He kept me on his back and started walking toward the middle of the park.

"Would you like me to walk?" I asked him.

"No, it's fine."

He was walking to the picnic tables. When he reached them he sat me on the top and then sat bellow me on the bench and leaned against my knees.

No one was around us. We were completely alone for the first time in a while. Ryan had his eyes closed. His brow was furrowed, which said he was thinking really hard about something. I'd never seen him like this, at least not this bad. He was debating on whether or not to say something.

"Ashlee, I . . . ." Ryan started.

I waited but he didn't say anything else.

"What is it? You can tell me." I said.

He stood up and got on the table top beside me. He put his arms around me and put his face by my ear.

"I love you." he whispered. "I know it took forever but I just didn't know how to tell you-"

I turned my head toward him and our lips met. He kissed me passionately for a minute and then I broke away.

"I love you, too." I breathed, he smiled.

"We should probably leave now." he said.

"Yeah."

Sigh.

"I'll walk you home."

He winked at me. He was going to come over later tonight, seeing as we had no more reason to watch Jafar twenty-four/seven.

I didn't like having night shift. She slept in a coffin. It really freaked me out, that's why Ryan started taking night shifts.

*   *   *

"Mom?" I said hesitantly.

We were making dinner and it would take at least four hours before it was ready.

"Yes, dear?" my mom replied.

"Um . . . can Ryan come over for dinner?"

"Of course! I love that kid!"

"Thanks, mom!"

I kissed her on the cheek and ran upstairs. My brother was waiting outside my door. He looked up when he heard me approach.

"What's up kid?" I asked.

"Oh. There you are! I wanted to know if I could do your make-up. Can I?" Duke rushed.

He had a habit of speaking fast. Too fast.

"Sure," I laughed, "come on in."

I opened the door and let him go in first, then I walked in. Duke was standing by my make-up. I walked over to him and sat in front of the mirror.

"Why exactly do you want to do this?" I asked him.

"Because my friends were bragging about how their sisters let them do their make-up and I've never done yours." Duke answered.

"Okay. Can I write a note first?"

"Sure."

"Thanks, Duke."

I got a piece of paper and my favorite pen. I started writing:

Ryan,

Hey could you come over for dinner? Mom already said you could if your mom said it was okay.

—Ashlee

P.S.

I love you.

I folded the paper in half then pressed a button on my cell which paged the kid that gives Ryan and my notes to each other.

"Could you go give this to the boy at the door?" I begged Duke.

"Sure." he took it and ran down he stairs.

I just sat there and waited. He was back in half a minute.

"May I start now?" he asked as he walked in the door.

"Yes."

He did my make-up and wouldn't let me look in the mirror until he was done. It felt like forever!

When he was finally done I jumped up and looked in the mirror. My mouth fell open.

"How'd I do?" Duke asked nervously.

"GREAT!"

"Really?"

"Yeah! Totally!"

"So do you like it?"

"Yeah! It's awesome!"

"Woohoo!"

There was a knock on the door at that second.

"That's Ryan." Duke said.

I wasn't listening; I was still looking in the mirror. I wondered if he could do my hair.

"Hey, Duke, you think you can do my hair?" I asked.

"Sure." he smiled.

And he started working on it.

"Ashlee! Ryan's here!" my mom shouted.

"I know! I'll be down in a few." I yelled back.

"Okay."

Duke finished my hair and I looked at it in the mirror. It was all curly and my front sides were pinned up with diamond flowers.

"Wow!" I cried, "I love it!"

"I'll pick out your outfit."

"Okay."

Duke walked over to one of my two closets. The one I never got in but it had the greater amount of clothes in it.

He picked out a casual blue, frilled dress that matched my make-up and the diamonds in my hair. Then he picked a pair of blue flats, he knew I didn't like heels. The flats had little jewels in the shape of flowers.

"Awesome choice my brother." I congratulated him.

"I'll go out and stand by the door. Just come out when you're done."

I dressed in the outfit he had picked and walked out the door after glancing in the mirror. The blue material clung to my figure.

My brother clapped when he saw me.

"You look awesome!" he shouted.

"Thanks. Oh my gosh! Looking this good makes me hungry. Let's go eat."

"Okay."

We walked into the kitchen. But we didn't just walk. We did it his way. He went in first and announced me.

"Introducing the styling of Adam Teaford! Modeling for us is my sister Ashlee!" he said like I was a runway model.

I walked in and cocked my hip, placing my hand on it. I glared.

"Oh! You look so pretty!" my mom exclaimed.

"Yeah, totally!" Ryan agreed.

"He did my make-up, my hair, and picked out my clothes." I said.

"Well, he did a good job!" mom cried.

"Where's dad?"

"Oh, he's still at work." mom sighed.

"Can we eat now?" Duke whined.

"Yes, Duke."

We all sat down at the table and ate; Ryan held my hand under the table.

After dinner we all went into the downstairs family room. Ryan and I helped my mom frame and hang pictures while my brother took a nap on the couch. After we were done hanging pictures I jumped on the couch to wake up Duke. He jerked awake and fell on the floor. I started laughing and everyone else joined, including Duke.

"Um . . . I think I should be getting home now, it's getting late." Ryan said after we all had stopped laughing.

"Yeah, I'll walk you home." I sighed.

"Can I come with you guys?" Duke begged.

"Sure kid." Ryan smiled.

"Hold on, I'll be right back." Duke ran upstairs.

He came back with a blue wrap. The exact same shade of blue as my dress. He walked up to me and had me bend down to his height so he could drape the wrap around my shoulders.

"That looks great." Ryan complimented, looking into my eyes.

I smiled.

Ryan, Duke, and I walked out the door and started walking down the street. Ryan took my hand; Duke was walking on my other side. I'd never actually been to Ryan's house. When we would get close to his house he would kiss me good-bye and say that he could walk alone the rest of the way. And we always stopped at the same spot.

We were in that spot now. He turned to me and Duke turned away from us, he knew what was coming.

Ryan and I leaned toward each other and kissed briefly. Then he pulled me into his arms and whispered in my ear.

"You look beautiful," he whispered, "but you look beautiful without the make-up and fancy clothes."

"Thanks." I kissed him on the cheek.

He was the same height as me now. He grew really fast. In about a week he would probably be two inches taller than me.

"I'll walk the rest of the way by myself," he said to Duke and me, "bye."

He held his fist out to my brother. They fist-bumped, Ryan kissed me on the cheek, and then he left.

"Come on, Duke." I said.

I put my arm around his shoulders.

"Can I ask you something, sis?" Duke hesitated.

"Sure. What is it?"

"Have you ever been to Ryan's house?"

"No. I haven't. Why?"

"I just wanted to know. You guys always stop there when I'm with you."

"He always does that."

"Why?"

"I haven't the slightest idea."

We were right in front of my house when I felt someone watching us. I looked down at Duke. He looked uncomfortable. I stopped and bent down in front of him.

"Do you have the feeling someone is watching us?" I whispered almost inaudibly.

He nodded.

I looked past his head and saw Jafar sitting in the bushes watching us. I pretended not to see her.

"Okay. Well, let's get inside." I muttered.

I picked him up and carried him through the door. My mom looked at me funny when she saw Duke in my arms. And I noticed that he was oddly light for a seven-year-old.

"I haven't seen you carry him since he was three," she said amused. "What's up?"

"I just felt like carrying him." I said casually and calmly.

"Okay."

"Could you hold on a second? I have to go do something in the kitchen."

"Is everything okay?" she asked suspiciously.

"Yeah, totally."

I walked into the kitchen with Duke still clinging to my side. I sat him down on the counter.

"You can't tell mom about what happened in front of the house. And please try to act normal." I told him.

"Okay, sis, I'll try." he whispered.

"Okay."

I picked him back up and put him on my side. Then I walked back in the living room where my mom was sitting in a chair reading her book. It looked like she was reading *Pride and Prejudice* again. I looked at the clock, it was seven thirty.

"I'm going to put Duke in bed." I told my mother.

"Okay." she replied, barely looking up from her book.

I carried him to his room and sat him on his bed.

"Good-night kid." I said sweetly.

"Can you leave the light on?" he whispered.

"You haven't done that since you were four, but okay."

"Thanks."

I left his room and went to mine. I felt someone standing behind me, by my door. I was thinking about screaming when a hand covered my mouth.

"It's just me." a voice whispered in my ear.

"Ryan!" I mumbled against his hand.

I turned and wrapped my arms around his waist. He kicked the door shut, lifted me up and carried me to my bed.

"Ashlee, we can't talk too loud," Ryan whispered, "Jafar is . . ."

"Right outside. I know." I breathed.

Ryan sat down beside me.

"Can I turn your stereo on?" he asked.

"Sure. But it's a bunch of Mozart and Beethoven. Slow songs."

"Perfect."

He reached over and turned it on then stood up in front of me with his hand out. I took it and stood. We waltzed around the room.

We had danced around for hours. I picked up Ryan's left hand and looked at his watch; it was 12:31 a.m.

"I have something for you." he said.

He stepped away from me, reached into his jacket pocket and withdrew a black, velvet box. It was the type of box that you get when you buy jewelry. He handed it to me.

I opened the box slowly. In it was a necklace covered in *real* emeralds. I could tell they were real; after all I am a rich girl.

"Oh my gosh! I love it! It's beautiful!" I shrieked.

"I'm glad you like it. It looks really great with your eyes." he smiled.

I started to put it on but he stopped me.

"Oh, here let me do that for you." he said.

I handed him the necklace and turned around. He lifted it over my head, I held my hair up and he clasped the necklace.

I looked down at it sparkling on my chest. It was really pretty. Nobody had ever given me something so nice. I started to cry.

"Are you alright?" Ryan asked anxiously.

"Yeah. It's just . . ."

"Happy crying?"

"Yeah."

I reached up around his neck and hugged him. All of a sudden he reached down and put his arm behind my knees and picked me up. I blushed and looked away.

He carried me to my purple bucket chair and sat down; I was sitting on his lap. The chair was big enough for two people so I moved to sit beside him; he scooted over to give me room.

We were facing each other. His hand on my cheek. I fell asleep.

*   *   *

I woke up and felt the weight of Ryan's hand on my cheek. Expecting him to be awake too, I opened my eyes. But his were shut. I heard a tiny snore.

"Aww!" I giggled, "that's so cute!"

He snored again.

I picked up his hand and put it beside him. I got up and stretched my hands above my head, as I did so I saw the light of my clock. It was 5:43 a.m. I looked down at Ryan, who snored again when I did.

I walked over to my dresser mirror and jumped when I saw my reflection. My make-up was smeared down my face. I looked hideous!

"Not completely hideous." a voice said behind me.

I turned around quickly. Ryan was standing by the wall, out of sight of the mirror. He smiled and winked at me. I couldn't help but to smile back.

"Good morning, Gorgeous. What's up?" he said.

I blushed.

"I'll help you get the make-up off if you want." he offered.

I nodded, went in my bathroom to get a wet washcloth, then came back and handed it to Ryan.

He was gentle and didn't miss any of it. It was like he had done it before. I didn't ask.

"So, I'm cute when I snore, huh?" he laughed.

"You were awake?"

"No. But I could still hear you and what you were thinking. When I heard you think you were hideous I woke up to tell you that you were wrong."

At that second I heard Duke getting out of his bed, then he mumbled something that sounded like 'birthday'. I looked over at my calendar and realized it *was* someone's birthday; Duke's! I hadn't realized how fast it had come. I didn't even have a present for him!

He was coming to my room to see if I knew what day it was. Then I had an idea; I'd act like I didn't know what day it was so I could throw him a surprise party. Brilliant! I knew all of his friends; they all hit on me, how hard could it be?

"What?" Ryan said appalled.

He had obviously been reading my mind, and he definitely didn't like the fact that a bunch of seven and eight-year-olds liked me. Cute insecurities.

"Nothing. Go hide under the bed." I giggled.

I fell into my big, purple bucket chair and pretended to be asleep. I heard snickering coming from under the bed. Apparently I wasn't very good in my attempts at acting. I heard my bedroom door open and the soft footsteps of my brother.

"Ashlee? Are you awake?" Duke whispered.

"No." I moaned.

"Oh, good you're up!"

"Didn't I just say I wasn't?"

"Yeah. But you answering in general tells me you're awake."

"Okay, good point. What do you need kid?" I said sitting up.

"Do you know what today is?"

"Monday?"

"Yes. And what else would it be?"

"November 22, 2010?"

"And . . . ?"

"Thanksgiving break."

"And . . . !?"

"I don't know."

"Oh. Okay, well, I'm going back to my room. Okay?"

"Alright."

He dropped his head and left the room, shutting the door behind him. Ryan came out from under the bed. He looked deep in thought. I looked away from him and walked over to my computer.

"What are you doing?" he asked as he sat down beside me.

"Emailing my brother's friends."

"Oh."

I could tell by the tone of his voice he didn't like the fact that I had little admirers and that they had my email address. It's not like he had any competition.

I made a list of Duke's friends in my head: Devin, Dean, Evan, Taylor, Eric, and Bananas. I don't know Bananas' real name and I didn't understand his nickname. Didn't really want to.

After I had emailed them I had to remember the name of the girl that Duke had a major crush on.

"It's Marie." Ryan told me.

"Thanks."

I emailed Marie and she responded a few seconds later saying that she wouldn't miss it. Now I just had to go to the mall and get Duke a present. When I say 'mall' it's not really a mall, just a few stores that are close to each other.

"Do you want to go to the mall with me?" I asked Ryan.

"Sure. I'll go home and change. I'll be back in ten minutes."

He climbed out the window.

I turned toward the closet I usually used then turned away and walked to the other one that had all the fancy clothes in it.

I walked in it and looked around at all the dresses. They were sorted by color and length. I went over to the line of green dresses.

I grabbed one that was mid-calf length and had a heart shaped emerald on it. It was frilled and creased all over, and it was strapless.

I took off the blue dress and pulled the green on over my head. I looked down at it as it swished around my legs.

I kicked off the blue shoes, which I was still wearing, over by the wall. As I did that I saw a wrap that was the exact same color as my dress. I pulled it off the hanger and put it on.

After finding a pair of shoes I left the closet and went downstairs for breakfast. My mom already had it on the table.

"That's a pretty dress." she complimented looking up.

"Thanks, mom."

"You're welcome. Your brother is upset that you forgot his birthday. You know?"

"Oh, I didn't forget. I'm just hiding the fact that I'm throwing him a surprise party.'

"Oh! Well that's sweet of you."

"Yeah. Speaking of . . . I need to go to the mall and buy his present. Ryan will be here in a minute to pick me up."

"Oh. Okay, go ahead. Have fun."

There was a knock on the door as she was talking, then Ryan walked into the kitchen.

"I let myself in. Is that all right?" he said.

"Of course. You two have fun at the mall." my mom smiled.

I took Ryan's hand and pulled him out the door. As soon as we were out of the house I was instantly aware of someone watching us. Jafar?

I looked at Ryan and he nodded. We kept walking and acted like we didn't know she was following us.

We had walked half way to the mall when Ryan stopped me. He looked like he had something on his mind. I looked into his eyes and waited for him to speak.

"That dress goes great with your necklace." he said.

"Thanks. But that's not what you were going to say."

"True. You know, you could just read my mind."

"But you know I don't like reading peoples' minds."

"I don't see why you don't read mine. I always read yours."

"I prefer when people tell me if they want to and I don't have to invade their privacy."

"I don't see how you live that way."

"You know you can tell me."

"Okay, fine. I was just wondering about the little kids that are hitting on you. It's nothing important, though."

"What about them?" I asked him skeptically.

"Can I kill them if they touch you at the party?"

"No! Plus you know I love you. And those kids are too young for me."

"Can I hold your hand at all times?"

"If it makes you feel better." I sighed.

"You know, if you didn't have a problem with reading peoples' minds we could have conversations that can't be overheard." he murmured and he winked.

I ignored it.

We continued walking to the mall. When we got there I saw a bunch of preps in the make-up aisle. I pulled Ryan the other way, toward the electronics. Duke needed a new laptop and he had never had a cell phone. He'd love to have those for his birthday.

We looked at all the phones and Ryan picked out the one I ended up buying; a black touch screen. Ryan knew what Duke would like because they were best friends now.

After buying an 'Apple' laptop we got out of there as fast as we could. And again, when we got outside Jafar started following us. Again.

We practically ran back to my house and when we got there we didn't walk right in. I poked my head in the door and looked around. I saw my mom walking into the kitchen.

"Mom!" I whispered.

"Oh, hello dear. I didn't notice you were back." she said startled.

"Where's Duke?"

"Upstairs in his room. It's safe to go up. Is Ryan still with you?"

"Yeah."

Ryan and I walked in the door. She was probably going to ask if Ryan was staying for dinner.

"Are you staying for dinner, Ryan dear?" she asked sweetly.

Right on cue.

"If it's not a bother." he responded.

I grabbed Ryan's hand and pulled him up the stairs. While my mom was still reassuring him, we walked into my room and shut the door. He didn't know it yet, but he was going to help me wrap the presents. Not really "wrap," though. More like stuff into a bag.

"You can wrap the cell phone." I said, handing it to him along with one of the birthday bags that I had already gotten out of my closet.

He slipped the phone into the bag and made the tissue paper puff up. I did the same with the laptop.

I looked at the clock. It was already 1:00pm. The party was set for 5:00pm. I had also bought decorations, so Ryan and I proceeded to decorate the backyard.

It was 4:00 by the time we had finished.

"Hey, guys! Come in here. Dinner is ready." my mom said from the backdoor.

"Has Duke been near the windows?" I asked.

"No. he's been helping me around the house."

She winked at me.

"Thanks mom." I laughed.

"Come in and eat."

We ate quickly. I watched Duke from across the table. He was picking at the pizza that he and my mom had made. There were tiny bits of pizza all over his plate.

Duke stood suddenly and walked to the sink.

"Aren't you hungry?" I asked.

"No, not really."

He dumped the food into the garbage disposal then went in the family room. I felt kind of bad; I'd never forgotten his birthday before. He must feel horrible and he's probably thinking I don't care about him anymore.

I looked at the clock on the wall. It announced that the time was 4:43pm. I heard a car outside. Ryan, my mom, and I got up and went to the door.

It was a car load of Duke's friends. It looked like Bananas, Evan, Eric, and Taylor. They all got out of the car, presents in hand, and walked toward us. Ryan grabbed my hand defensively.

"Ryan. You're the one who has to show them to the backyard." I whispered in his ear.

"Why me!?"

"Because I have to distract Duke. But I guess I could show them to . . ."

"Alright. I'll do it."

"Be nice."

At that he stuck his tongue out at me. He led the kids to the backyard. My mom had ran off to the kitchen.

I walked into the living room and found Duke stretched out on the couch watching TV. I walked over and sat on the edge of the couch by his feet.

"Do you want to take a walk with me?" I asked him.

"Sure."

"Okay. But you have to change into different clothes."

"What's wrong with these?"

"Just change into something a little nicer."

"But we are just taking a walk. Do I really have to change?"

"Yes!"

"Fine."

He trudged up the stairs. When he came back down he was wearing a white button-up shirt and faded blue jeans.

"Great. Now we can go for that walk." I said.

"Alright. So is there anything important about today, Ashlee?"

"No. Not that I know of at least."

"Oh. Okay."

He sighed.

I looked out the window before we went out the door in case there was a car out there. There wasn't so I rushed Duke out the door and we started walking up the street. I felt so bad about making Duke sad. He didn't say much as we walked.

"You know that Marie girl? Do you still like her?" I asked, making conversation.

"Yeah. I still like her. You remembered that?"

"Of course I did."

"Okay. Well yeah, I still like her, but I don't know what to say to her."

"Just be yourself Adam. She'll like you for that. Plus you are awesome so who wouldn't like you?"

"Everyone."

"Okay, that was a rhetorical question. But what do you mean?"

"None of my friends have talked to me today."

"Had it crossed your mind that they might be busy?"

"Well, I actually didn't consider it."

"Then that's probably the case."

"I guess you're right."

"I'm always right."

"Sure you are."

Just then my phone vibrated. I took it out of the pocket on the side of my dress. It had a message from Ryan. He said that everyone was there now and to come back.

"Do you want to go back home now, Duke?"

"Sure."

We walked home quickly, Duke practically running to keep up but he never said anything. We got there in five minutes. He started toward the door but I grabbed his hand.

"This way Duke." I said.

"Why?" he sighed.

"I have something for you in the backyard."

"Fine."

We walked through the back gate.

"SURPRISE!" everyone shouted.

They all ran to greet Duke. He did truly look surprised.

"You didn't think I'd forget your birthday, did you?" I laughed.

I walked over to Ryan as the crowd of kids swallowed Duke. Ryan automatically took my hand, almost absentmindedly. But he was to alert to be doing things absentmindedly.

"What is it?" I asked him, thinking it was Jafar.

"No. It's not her. She's not even here right now. Something just feels off. It feels like something's going to happen. Tonight."

As he said this, the feeling, the atmosphere, of the backyard devoured me. It was exactly

like he had said. I could feel it more than him
though. I knew who it was going to happen
to and what time it was going to happen. The
only thing I didn't know was what was going
to happen.

"It's going to happen to Duke at midnight."
I whispered mechanically.

"What's going to happen?" Ryan asked,
squeezing my hand.

"I don't know."

"Well, we will have to pretend to have fun
and hide our worry. We want this party to
make Duke happy."

"Okay."

As the party continued, Duke's smile got
bigger an bigger by the second. He got to cut
his cake, got to eat the first piece, and the girl
he liked never left his side. Then, finally, at
6:50 he opened his presents, thanked everyone
a thousand times, and then by 7:00 everyone
was gone. The backyard was empty besides
Duke, Ryan, my mom, and me. My mom told
us to go in the house and she would clean up.

We all went up to my room. Duke laid on
the floor, I sat on the end of my couch, and

Ryan laid on the couch with his head on my lap. We watched TV for four hours. Then my mom walked in.

"Ryan, since it's already eleven-o-clock would you like to stay the night? You could sleep in the guest room." she said.

"Umm sure. Sorry, I didn't know it had gotten late or I would have gone home." Ryan answered, head still in my lap.

"It's no problem. I'll call your mom and tell her."

"Alright."

My mom left the room and we all resumed watching the cartoon my brother had picked. I noticed it was still kind of light outside. I got up and walked toward the window. When I put my hand on the curtain to yank it back I had another weird feeling. Stronger than before. If I was to open the curtain it would quicken what was going to happen, it would make it happen now.

I let go of the curtain and sat back down. Ryan and Duke both looked at me with an odd expression, Ryan's became understanding as he read my mind. Duke just turned back to the TV.

I kept nervously watching the clock and Duke, waiting for it to happen. It was ten till twelve when my mom came in to tell us all to get in bed. The two boys left my room and so did my mom. I didn't move, I just stayed on my couch and watched the minutes go by. The guest room was right beside mine, so when the clock hit twelve I could knock on the wall.

It was eleven fifty-eight when my brother came into my room clutching his stomach. I got up and ran to him.

"Are you okay?" I gasped.

"I . . . I don't know . . . what's happening. My stomach . . . hurts." he told me. Then he gasped in pain.

I ran to the wall that was shared with the guest room and knocked on it. Tears were running down my face.

Ryan ran into the room and over to Duke. I joined them. Duke had fallen to the floor in the middle of my room. He curled into a ball on his side, holding his stomach.

Ryan and I both looked up as my clock chimed, signaling that it was midnight. I looked back down at the floor where my brother had been. I gasped in horror and Ryan looked down to see why. His mouth dropped open but no sound came out of it.

It was impossible that we were seeing correctly. I blinked a couple times but the thing I saw didn't change. And it wasn't like a dream, it was real. I couldn't wake up from this. And my brother could never escape it. He was doomed to this for the rest of his life.

I was wondering how this could be possible when Ryan came to my side and took my hand. He knew what this meant just as well as I did.

What I saw on my floor that used to be my brother was not human, but there was not a doubt in my mind that it *was* my brother.

CHAPTER 9
Werewolves

"Oh my gosh!" Ryan finally choked out.

"I know! I can't believe this." I mumbled.

I just stared at the wolf that was lying in the floor at my feet wondering why I'd never known about this. Might as well talk to Ryan through my thoughts, there's no way I'd be able to talk out loud.

This means that my dad is a werewolf, right? I thought toward Ryan.

Yes. I'm sorry you had to find out like this. It's horrible. Ryan thought back.

Well, I mostly feel bad for him. Think of how painful it must have been. I think I might be going into shock. Is that possible for a vampire?

Ashlee? You're a vampire? Duke's thought broke in.

Duke!? You can hear us? I said in my head, but all that came out of my mouth was a gasp.

I guess. Unless I'm hearing voices, which is possible. I'm more than a little confused right now.

Ashlee, you need to explain everything to your brother. And I mean every single *thing.* Ryan thought.

Right. Okay. Duke, Ryan and I are vampires. And you just became a werewolf. I tried keeping the explanation simple.

Actually, you're a werewolf because you were born with it. Ryan added.

That's why I've felt weird all day? I mentioned it to mom but she said it was just puberty. Ugh! Duke complained.

In a way, it is puberty. I guess. I've never really known any werewolves before.

Sarcasm. Great.

Way to be real Ryan. This is serious. I sighed mentally.

Sorry. You're right, this is serious. And now that this has happened I need to tell you about something that I've kept from both of you; why I've never taken either of you to my house.

What is it Ryan? my brother and I thought together.

"My mom is . . . she has a condition. She is what Adam is."

"What!?" I gasped.

What's wrong with that? Duke asked confused.

"Girls normally don't turn into werewolves, Duke. Unless . . ."

"They've been bitten by one." Ryan finished.

Oh. I see now. Look, I'm sorry, man. That must suck. Duke thought, understanding in his tone.

"Look who's talking wolf-boy." he joked, the wolf in the floor coughed a laugh in response. "Of course, there's more than just my mom. There's my dad."

He was completely serious now.

"What's wrong with your dad?"

"He's a vampire."

So? You and Ashlee are, too. What's the difference?

"He feeds . . . differently." he looked into my eyes.

"Oh." I choked out.

Oh my god. I didn't think about that. You guys murder people! Ugh! You suck the life right out of them!

"No, Duke, we don't. We suck the life out of animals. And now that you are a werewolf I think I'd rather starve." I sighed.

"Don't you just love how people jump to conclusions about our dietary habits? I think I'd rather starve now, too. It'd feel weird now that your *brother* is an animal." Ryan commented.

Now, you guys don't start that. Just 'cause I'm a dog *doesn't mean anything. Don't go and starve yourselves. Wait . . . you said your dad feeds differently, does that mean . . .*

"Yes. He feeds on . . . people" Ryan sighed, ashamed.

I reached up and touched his face. "I'm so sorry."

"It's all right. I mean not everyone is like us, though I know a lot of vampires who are."

Um . . . guys, I have a question. How long do I stay a wolf?

"All night." I answered before Ryan even opened his mouth.

Ryan stared at me confused.

"I have a friend that's a werewolf. I didn't think it was that important for you to know so I never told you."

"Who?" he sighed.

"Well, there's more than just one." I stalled.

"What!? How many?"

"Five. Maybe six."

"Who?"

"You knew one of them but you didn't really like them. I don't get why she got so mad when she found out I was hiding my being a vampire from her, she felt perfectly fine not telling me anything. Plus, you think she would have noticed."

"Karla? Really?"

"Yeah, and you know that Aaron kid in our second period class? And Tyler in fifth?"

"*They* are werewolves!?"

"Yeah. And Jeff from gym, Margret from computers, and most shockingly, our biology teacher, Mr. Watson."

"Wow. You think I would've noticed." Ryan mumbled, "their thought patterns are different than humans' and I've read Tyler's when he was trying to get me to . . . never mind." he caught my suspicious glance toward him. But he continued, "and I read Mr. Watson's mind because he was staring at me funny and I wanted to know why. Do you think they know about us?"

"I don't know. But what was that about Tyler?"

"It's . . . nothing. Don't worry, I didn't do anything. Trust me you would've been the first to know."

You said Karla was a werewolf right? Well, wasn't the bite marks on her neck from an animal? Do you think she could've got attacked again?

Ryan and I looked at each other with nervous expressions. We knew we had to tell him. Was there a way we could block our thoughts from my brother? Worth a shot.

I volunteer you to tell him. I thought directly to Ryan, trying as hard as I could to block Duke.

"Why don't you? He heard what you thought anyway."

She thought something? I didn't hear it.

"Seriously?" Ryan asked, looking at me with a confused expression.

"I did that on purpose. I thought it directly to you and blocked Duke. I wasn't sure it would work, but it did. So you can tell him."

Ryan hesitated.

"You could think it if that makes it easier." I suggested.

What are you guys going on about? Duke thought.

We killed Karla. Ryan's thought was a mental whisper.

What? Why?

She was going to expose us. I guess we kind of exposed ourselves.

No one would have believed her. They would have called her crazy.

She was going to have evidence.

As Ryan thought this he hissed.

What evidence?

Your sister. They would have killed her you know.

Duke started growling.

"Be quiet, Duke! You're going to wake mom up!" I hissed at him. He broke off in mid growl.

Sorry.

"It's alright kid. You'll get used to it." Ryan assured him.

How long do I stay like this? You know, the wolf form.

I looked at my alarm clock. 4:00 a.m. Sad thing is that most of our conversation took place in our heads.

"Probably one more hour." I answered.

"That's normally how it is for my mom."

Great. So is this every night or just full moon?

"Just full moon." Ryan and I said blankly.

For the rest of that hour we just stared at each other. I stared at Duke, Ryan stared at me, and Duke kept switching his gaze between me and Ryan, but he mostly watched me. I guessed that it was because I would actually meet his gaze; Ryan wouldn't take his eyes off of me long enough.

"It's five-o-clock." Ryan switched his gaze to my brother.

Duke was curled up in a ball sleeping now. He started glowing when Ryan spoke. It was a dim golden glow. You could see him changing back to a human.

His paws were first; they changed back to hands and feet. Then his legs, arms, and head. And, the last thing to change, his torso. He was my human brother again, well I guess half human.

He opened his eyes and looked at us curiously. Then looked down at himself.

"I'm human!" he whispered excitedly.

"Half" Ryan said in a pained voice.

I started walking toward him and he opened his arms for me. I went into them and wrapped mine around his waist. He put one hand on the back of my head, holding it to his chest; the other hand was between my shoulder blades.

"Aw guys! C'mon, I'm still in the room. Ugh!" Duke whined.

Ryan pulled my face up and put his lips to mine. This brought many more complaints from my brother.

"If it bothers you, go back to your own room." Ryan mumbled against my lips.

I didn't look up to watch him leave, but I heard the door open and close.

Ryan picked me up and sat down in my bucket chair, not once taking his lips off mine. I was sitting on his lap like last time, but this time I didn't slide off to sit beside him. I don't think he would have let me anyway.

We sat there, though we had stopped kissing. I stayed on his lap and nestled my face into his chest. We both fell asleep.

*　　*　　*

"Ashlee! Wake up! You got to see this! Wake up!" Duke was shouting.

I realized I was lying down and that Ryan wasn't holding me. I opened my eyes and looked around. I was in my bed; Ryan must've put me in my bed and went back to the guest room.

"Ashlee, read this." my brother said shoving a newspaper at me and knocking on the wall conjoining my room and the guest room.

Ryan came running in. He wasn't wearing a shirt but he was still in his jeans. Why didn't he borrow a pair of lounging pants?

"What? What's going on?" Ryan said rubbing his eyes.

"You two have to read that." Duke was pointing at the newspaper.

Ryan came over and sat on the bed. I handed the paper to him. He looked up at me.

"Read it out loud. I'm not much of a morning person."

He smiled at me. "I'm not reading it out loud. Read it over my shoulder. I'm not a morning person either."

I moved so I was standing on my knees behind him.

We both read the short article:

Police Investigators Have a Clue!

All those older people out there. Remember a time, not long ago. A time when everyone believed in vampires. When you

would never leave the house without garlic.

Well, brake out the garlic again. Investigators report that the animal that attacked young Karla Case was no ordinary animal. The puncture mark was shaped almost the same as human teeth. The investigators took a saliva swab from the wound and found that it was not saliva at all.

What looked like saliva was actually venom. Venom that ate through a sheet of metal in the lab.

So wherever you go, have garlic on you and don't be out in the dark without a wooden stake.

Ryan and I looked up into each other's eyes. Though it was funny that they thought garlic would keep us away and a wooden stake is all that would kill us, we were going to die.

The vampire media would find us, then they would tell the Royals and they would have us executed.

"What do we do Ryan?" I asked, I couldn't even hear myself say the words.

Ryan just stared at me. Duke stared at us both waiting for us to react more, waiting for Ryan to answer my question.

"Ryan? Are you gonna answer man, or just sit there?" Duke whispered.

"I'm trying to think. I don't know what to do. We can't run, we can't hide. Alex is looking for us and wants us to join him. When we tell him no, that will lead to a fight." Ryan debated.

"Wait, who is Alex?" Duke asked with a confused look on his face.

"The guy who made us vampires." Ryan answered blankly.

"And what's his problem?"

"He's evil and wants us to help him create other evil vampires. He's a major lunatic. He wants to create a world of all vampires. I just got an idea!"

"What is it?" I asked.

"You know when we tell him we don't want join him he's going to go off and make a bunch of new vamps. People are going to notice his little massacre. He and his minions will have to feed."

"And we can blame him?"

"Sort of. But first we need to contact some friends from our supernatural world."

"I'll help!" Duke offered.

"No!" I cried.

"Ashlee . . ." Ryan hesitated.

"No, you can't be serious. You're actually considering it?"

"Ashlee, we need all the help we can get."

"Not my brother. He's not getting involved in this."

"Be reasonable . . ."

"He's not your brother! You don't get it."

"Ash . . . I want to." Duke said.

"I don't want to lose my brother Ryan." I ignored Duke.

"I'm not going to argue with you. It's Adam's decision."

We looked at my brother. I knew what the answer was. I didn't even let him say it.

"Fine. Go ahead and risk your life Adam."

"Ash, I'm trying to protect yours." Duke said.

Ryan stood up and walked over to my computer. He turned it on and the startup password popped up.

"The password is on the sticky note by the mouse." I told him.

He gave me a thumbs up and typed it in. When it was done logging on he went on the internet.

"What are you doing?" I asked.

"I'm getting on my email. I'm going to talk to other supernatural creatures of the world and see if they will help us."

He typed fast. Never looking away from the screen. Duke sat down on the bed and put his head on my lap. I rubbed his shoulder.

"I'm sorry Ashlee." he said.

I knew that meant, 'I'm sorry that you are upset, but I'm still going to risk my life for the sake of yours.'

"Yes!" Ryan shouted.

"Ry, be quiet! What is it?" I said softly.

"Sorry. But I got a few people to help."

"Who?"

"Two warlocks and a witch."

"Okay. Go on my email now."

"I just did. Hold on, I have a couple people who just answered."

"Who was it?"

"A genie, another warlock, three vamps, and a ghost."

"Awesome. So altogether that's nine people."

"Actually, twelve people. You left out the three of us."

"Okay fine. Twelve, or nine, it's still not enough."

"I know."

"So who else can we ask?"

"Can you get me a phone book? I have some calls to make."

"We don't get long distance."

"I never said they were long distance. No, they are local."

Duke got up and got the phone book off my dresser. He handed it to Ryan. Ryan grabbed the phone off my desk. He dialed the number and waited. He didn't want to put it on speaker phone.

I heard a lady answer.

"Hello. Is Tyler there?" pause "It's Ryan."

"You're asking Tyler for a favor!?" I hissed.

I heard Tyler on the phone.

"Hi Tyler. I have to talk to you about something serious . . . no I didn't . . . . I told you I wasn't going to . . . look Tyler . . . no . . . look I know you are a werewolf . . . because I'm a vampire . . . . we need your help . . . . a fight . . . thanks. Bye."

"What was that?" I asked.

"He's helping."

"Tyler? Helping? Well, he never misses a fight."

Ryan dialed another number and put the phone to his ear.

A boy answered.

"Hey, Aaron . . . I'm not so good . . . . okay . . . I already told Tyler no . . . look I know you are a werewolf and I need your help . . . yes I'm a vampire . . . in a fight . . . really? Thanks . . . get as many as you can . . . thanks again. Bye."

"That was fast."

"He knows a lot of people who would love to help. He will call back and he wants to help too."

Ryan called Jeff then Margret. Jeff said he'd love to shred some vamps and Margret was won over by just the sound of Ryan's voice.

The phone rang right after Ryan was done talking to Margret.

"Hello? . . . oh, hey Aaron. What do you have? . . . . five? Really? . . . that's amazing . . . names? . . . John, Paul, Mr. Watson, Lynette, and Sandy? . . . okay . . . yeah I wrote them down . . . that's all you could get? . . . . okay that's fine . . . thanks for everything. Bye."

"Two girls and three guys." I commented.

"Yeah. That kid just saved me from calling a teacher."

"You must be so grateful."

"Funny. How many we got?"

"Twenty-one."

"If we hadn't killed Karla we could have asked her."

"If we hadn't killed Karla we wouldn't be in this mess."

I started crying. Ryan came over and held me in his arms. Duke took one of my hands and held it.

I wish Karla was a bloodstain I could just mop up and it would be like there was never a stain. But that wouldn't happen. Karla's bloodstain was on my life forever. And I was scarred with it. Not even Ryan could shield me from the pain of it.

As hard as he tries he knows he can't block her out. Just like I can't. The blood shed was on both of our hands. And I knew he didn't want it to be on mine, but not even he can change the past. As much as he wanted to, it was impossible. We were stained for life.

Just this once I wanted to read his mind. To know what he was thinking. I didn't want to invade his privacy but I wanted to know.

I reached out with my mind and listened to his thoughts.

Why did I help her kill Karla? I should have told her it wasn't worth it then went to Karla's and killed her myself. Dispose of the evidence, my dad told me all the time! Why didn't I remember that then? I was so distracted by

Ashlee . . . ah Ashlee, why would Tyler want me to dig up sick lies about her? Well, I know why, but it is disturbing. That kid is a real weirdo. And getting Aaron to help him, what the heck is he thinking? That I'll fall under peer pressure? I love Ashlee too much for that, more than my own life.

"I love you Ash." Ryan sighed.

More than your own life, don't forget that. I cried harder.

CHAPTER 10
An Unexpected Arrival

Ryan had gone home a few hours ago. Duke went down stairs to eat. I stayed up in my room on the vampire internet looking for good vampires that could help us and emailed them. Four of them said they would help the others said they'd love to but they weren't available. The four that said they'd help also told me they would talk to their friends. One of the four said they had two friends that would help; the remaining three said their friends didn't want to take part in a fight.

So we now had our numbers standing at twenty-seven. Unless Ryan got more people too.

I got out a sheet of paper and wrote a note for Ryan.

Ryan,

As far as I know, our numbers stand at twenty-seven. I got a few people off the vamp-net. Did you get anyone else? And I still don't feel comfortable that my brother is involved in this.

-Ashlee

P.S. Are you able to come over?

I pushed the button on my cell and then I took the note down stairs to the door and gave it to the kid who delivers our notes.

I went straight back upstairs and laid on my bed, listening for the doorbell. When I heard it I didn't move, I was half asleep. My mom brought the note up and laid it by my arm and left the room. I got up and read the note:

Ashlee,

I didn't get anyone else. Yeah I can come over; I'll be there in ten minutes.

-Ryan

P.S. Love you.

"Mom, Ryan's coming over" I shouted downstairs.

She didn't respond. I got up and went to the door.

"Mom?" still no answer.

I walked down the hall to her bedroom.

"Mom? Dad?" nothing.

Maybe Duke knew where they were. I walked down the hall to his bedroom; the door was open so I walked in. I didn't see him anywhere; I walked over to his bathroom and knocked on the door.

"Duke? Are you in there?" no one answered.

I opened the door, the bathroom was empty.

"Ashlee, where's your family?" a voice said behind me.

I turned around fast. I knew it was Ryan, I knew his voice. But I was still a little jumpy. My family just up and disappeared.

"Sorry. I did knock, five times actually." he walked over to me and wrapped his arms around my shoulders.

"It's okay. I was looking for everyone; I didn't even hear you knock. Is the car out there?" I said into his chest.

"I'll go check."

And he disappeared. I almost fell on my face but he caught me before I could.

"Yeah, the car is out there." he said.

"Where are they then?"

"I didn't see them in the backyard either."

"What the heck?"

I pulled away from him, grabbed his hand, and walked out the door to the stairs. I stopped at the top.

"What?" Ryan asked.

I was staring at a wall which kind of alarmed him.

"There was a painting here. It was my mom's favorite; she would never take it down unless she was cleaning it."

"So . . . ."

"She cleaned it yesterday."

I pulled Ryan downstairs into the kitchen. When we walked in the kitchen I found the painting. It was leaning against the microwave with a note on it. I grabbed the note and Ryan moved behind me so he could read over my shoulder.

Ashlee and Ryan,

Ashlee's family, as you have noticed, is gone. Meet me at the enclosed address. Bring no one with you. I'll know if you do. I'm a vampire like you. Ashlee, take your family's car, write a note that says you all went to a relative's house, and stick the note on your front door.

I'll see you later.

"So my family got kidnapped?" I whispered.

"Maybe."

"We're going to go get them?"

"Yep."

"Wait, I can't drive."

"Nope. But I can."

"Let's go." I got a piece of paper.

"What's that for?"

"I have to write the note." I wrote as I spoke.

I went and got the tape and taped the note to the door.

"C'mon Ryan." I said grabbing the keys.

He followed me out the door. I tossed the keys to him and got in the passenger seat. He got in and started the car. He looked at me and held out his hand. I gave him the note with the address facing up. He pulled the car out of the driveway.

"Do you know where this is?" he asked.

I looked at the address.

"Yeah. It's the street the school is on." I told him.

He started driving toward the school. As we were driving I was thinking of worst case scenarios. He was going to kill them. Alex was going to kill them. My dad and brother wouldn't be freaked out by a vampire, but my mom would. She didn't know about the supernatural world, of all the supposedly mythical creatures. She'd have a heart attack; Alex wouldn't have to worry about killing her.

"How do you know it's Alex?" Ryan said taking my hand.

"It's not hard to guess. This is his way of making us join him. How are we going to say no with him being able to kill my family?"

"You don't exactly know it's him, you're just guessing. And if it is him, you don't know he's going to kill them."

KAYLA N. DEMPSEY

"Just drive." I took my hand out of his.

"You're still mad about your brother being involved, aren't you?"

"Ryan, my whole family is involved now."

"You don't know that. It could be someone else."

"It's most likely him though."

"'Most likely' which means there's a chance it's someone else. Ashlee, you need to calm down . . ."

"Never tell a girl to calm down! That only makes it worse."

"Okay, sorry."

We drove in silence. It wasn't until the school came into sight that we spoke again.

"Where now?" Ryan asked me.

"Turn right at the school. It's a dead end street. And this address is the last house on it."

"Okay. And don't worry, they'll be fine."

I didn't answer. How could he possibly know? He can't see the future he can only see the past.

"That's it!" Ryan exclaimed.

"What?"

"Take the wheel."

"Um . . ."

"Just take it."

"Okay."

I grabbed it but he let go of it before I could so I had to get the car back on the road. He closed his eyes for a few minutes.

"Ryan?" I said.

He opened his eyes smiling.

"Yes?" he answered. He took the wheel back.

"What was that about?"

"I was checking the past."

"And . . . ?"

"And it wasn't Alex. Your family wasn't kidnapped. They aren't going to die."

"So who was it?"

"I can't tell you. It's a surprise."

"Come on." I whined.

I grabbed his arm and leaned on his shoulder with my face by his. He looked at me out of the corner of his eye. He frowned at my sad face and looked away.

"I can't tell you. It will ruin the surprise for you." he whispered.

I kissed his cheek and batted my eyelashes. I know he saw because his breath caught.

"Which side of the street is it on?"

I sighed.

"It's right there Ryan. Pull in the driveway." I said scooting away from him.

He put his arm around my shoulders and held me to him.

"I can't get in the driveway." he told me.

I looked up at him, then at the drive way. There was a car in it. But I knew this car. Ryan let go of me and got out of the car. He came around and opened my door. When I got out he put his arm around my shoulders again. He pulled me toward the door.

He didn't bother knocking he just opened the door. It was dark so I was on my guard, ready to fight. Ryan laughed.

"It's okay." he whispered in my ear.

He flipped the lights on. When he did I saw my whole family. And I do mean my *whole* family.

"Oh my gosh!" I shrieked.

"Surprise. Hey sis!" my older sister laughed. She held her arms open.

"Holy crap! Grace!" I jumped into her arms.

She laughed at me. I had missed that laugh. She'd been gone for years. She's probably only back for the weekend or something.

"How long are you staying?" I asked her.

"A while." she answered.

I pulled away and went back to Ryan. He put his arm around me again. I looked up at Grace.

"What's with the weird look?" she asked me.

"How long is a while?" I ignored her question.

"Well, I actually bought this house, so I guess a few years or so. Maybe more."

I smiled at her. She had a way of letting me freak before telling me the truth. Then I freak even more because the truth is awesome.

Just then I was trying hard to remember something but I couldn't. What was it? It had something to do with the note my sister left.

Ryan moved behind me and put his arms around my chest, putting his chin on my shoulder.

"Does it have to do with the fact that your sister knows that you are a vampire and that *she* is one?" he whispered so low I could barely hear him.

That was it! Man I love my crazy boyfriend.

"I know. I love you, too. My crazy girlfriend." he chuckled.

I turned my and kissed him on the cheek. He blushed. He knows I never show that much affection to him when we were with my parents.

My sister was watching us, smiling. I missed that smile too. Grace was really pretty. The only one in my family with black hair, but she makes it work. When she left for California five years ago she had had a great tan, now she was horribly pale. And her eyes had gotten brighter. It sucks being turned. How old was she now? Twenty?

Grace shook her head and then mouthed "twenty-three." She was still smiling. I looked at Ryan. He nodded and took his arms off me. I walked over to my sister.

"Can I talk to you alone?" I said in a rushed whisper.

She took my hand and pulled me into the kitchen.

"Go ahead." she said after shutting the door.

She hopped up on the counter and crossed her legs against the cabinet. I moved toward her and leaned on the counter beside her.

"You're a vampire?" I asked.

"Yes."

"That's how you know I'm one?"

"Sort of."

"What's that supposed to mean?"

"I have a few vamp friends. You talked to them on the internet. They remembered me talking about you and told me about your . . . situation. Do you need more help?"

No! Not her too. I already hated it that Duke was involved.

Ryan walked in the kitchen then. He had that look on his face.

"No Ryan. Not her too." I glared at him.

"We need all the help we can get. It's her choice."

"No."

"Ash . . ."

"No Ryan!"

"Shhh! Don't be too loud. There are people in the other room."

"Sorry. She's not helping."

"Ashlee, I will help. I'm older than you. You can't treat me like Duke." Grace cut in.

"So would you like to help us?" Ryan asked her, ignoring me.

"Yes. And what did she mean when she said 'not her *too*?'"

"Duke is helping us."

"What!? He is a little human boy! How's he supposed to help?"

"No. He's not." I said flatly.

"What are you talking about Ashlee?" Grace turned all of her attention on me.

"Duke is only half human. He's a werewolf."

"What? No. That can't be. It's not possible. That would mean that dad is . . . ."

"Yeah. I know."

"What the heck?"

"Yeah."

She looked out of the front kitchen window and apparently saw the family car.

"You can't drive." she said suddenly.

"Nope."

"And you drove anyway!?"

"Nope."

"Then how'd you get here?"

I pointed at Ryan.

"Oh. I see. Boyfriend?"

"Yep."

"No introductions?"

"Sorry. Grace this is Ryan. He's a vampire too."

"Okay, I wasn't sure about the vampire thing."

Ryan came over to me and put his arm around my shoulder. I smacked him and he laughed. He picked me up and threw me over his shoulder.

"Ryan!" I screamed.

Grace was about to fall of the counter because she was laughing so hard. And I could feel Ryan laughing underneath me. The laughter was so contagious that I joined in.

"What's going on in here?" I heard my mom come in the room.

"Hi mom." Grace said, still laughing.

My mom joined in laughing too. Duke and my dad walked in the room then and also started laughing.

Ryan finally put me down. And everyone was still laughing. Ryan turned to my brother, his back to me. I caught my bro's eye and told him to move over a little. He did. I jumped and landed on Ryan's back.

He definitely wasn't expecting it because he fell to the floor and everyone laughed harder. Including him. He shifted and I lay there across his stomach unable to get up from laughing so hard.

It was like a family laughing contest. I was the first to stop laughing, then Ryan. My face was right above his. He did something I never thought he would do in front of my parents.

He reached up and held my face with both hands. A mischievous gleam in his eyes. He leaned up slowly and put his lips on mine. I froze. Everyone had stopped laughing. They were probably all staring now.

"Awwww!" everyone sighed, as if it was the most adorable thing they have ever seen.

And they burst into applause.

Ryan broke away from me and laughed at the look on my face. I could feel that my face was hot so I knew I was blushing. I smiled at him.

He sat up which left me laying on his lap, then pulled me up to a sitting position on his lap.

"Hey, Grace! Got any presents for us?" Duke said suddenly.

"Duke!" I said, "that's so impolite."

"Well, somebody's gotten more proper since the last time I've seen them." Grace chuckled at me.

I stuck my tongue out at her.

"Either way, yeah I have presents." she continued.

"Cool! What did you get me?" Duke said, bouncing on his toes.

"They're in the other room. Everybody can go in there and I'll be right out. I need to talk to Ashlee and Ryan first."

"Ugh. Fine." with that being said he turned on his heel and left the room.

My parents followed him out. I turned and faced my sister. I was still sitting on Ryan's lap in the middle of the kitchen floor. I held my hand out toward Grace and she lifted me up.

Ryan was standing erect beside me as soon as I was off of him.

I hated vampire movement I preferred to move like a slow human, it's more comfortable. Then again, I'm the weirdest vampire ever created.

"No you're not. You're the most beautiful, normal, loving vampire that has ever existed." Ryan said grabbing my hand.

"What? That was random." Grace said confused.

"No it wasn't. He just responded to my thoughts." I raised an eyebrow at her.

"How could he possibly 'respond to your thoughts' Ash? That's impossible."

"Really? He can read minds."

"Shut up. Really?"

"Yeah, I can too."

"How come I can't?"

"You can't?"

"Nope."

I looked at Ryan. He shrugged. *Is it so normal now, Ryan?* He told me it was normal for a vamp to read minds.

"Hey, now. Don't go accusing. I thought it was the vamp norm." he said quietly.

"None of my vamp friends can read minds either. Trust me, if we could we would have perfect grades in college, we'd get called nerds and not care." Grace informed us.

I looked at her then back at Ryan.

"Okay. I don't think I understand the vampire norm anymore. I don't think I want to either." he mumbled, more or less, to himself.

"Wait, if you can't read minds, how did you know I was trying to remember how old you were." I asked, suddenly remembering that crucial piece of information.

"I can't read minds, but I can read lips. You were practically speaking your thoughts. Just without audio. I'm not stupid. And, if you could read minds, wouldn't you be able to know that?"

"She doesn't use her abilities unless absolutely necessary. She thinks it's wrong to invade peoples' privacy. Even humans. My crazy, weird, beautiful, *normal* girlfriend." Ryan said for me.

"Well, my crazy, wonderful, hot, *normal* boyfriend. I love you, too." I giggled.

"Wow. You two are so gonna get married." Grace said.

Okay. Random. But then again we were in the presence of the most random person (vampire or human) alive or dead. Whatever we are.

Getting married? My sister brings up the weirdest things. My crazy, erratic sister. Man, I had missed the randomness.

Ryan laughed. It was a tight laugh with barely any humor. I looked up at him. He had a crease between his brows as if I'd offended him with my laughing at marriage in my mind.

Then I realized it was just that. He was offended, not by me laughing at marriage in general, but rather by the fact I found it ludicrous, utterly absurd, that my sister would think that of us.

Blocking my thoughts so that Ryan couldn't hear them, I debated about marriage. And soon after I started thinking of it, I wanted it. And bad. I actually wanted, no, needed to marry Ryan. If not, how could I know he was truly mine? And marriage would take our relationship a step farther. And I really wanted to take that step. I wanted it so much it was painful. Thanks a lot Grace.

CHAPTER 11
Commitment

"So did you have fun seeing your sister?" Ryan asked.

He was lying across my bed watching me write a list of "people" that were helping us. I was wearing the emerald bracelet that Grace had gotten me.

"Yes." I answered not looking up.

"That's all I'm going to get?"

I didn't respond.

"Okay. Well, can you read the list?"

I held the paper up and read from it:

"Vampires:
Jenny: age 20, blue eyes, brown hair, 5'3"
Johnson: age17, green eyes, red hair, 6'0"
Vlad: age 25, black eyes, black hair, 7'2"

Kelsey: age 19, blue/green eyes, blonde
  hair, 5'7"
Jostlen: age 18, silver eyes, white hair, 5'0"
Stefan: age 18, blue eyes, black hair, 6'3"
Chelsea: age 16, green eyes, black hair, 5'7"
Ashlee: age 15, brown eyes, brown hair, 5'8"
Ryan: age 16, blue eyes, brown/blonde hair,
  5'10"
Grace: age 23, brown eyes, black hair, 5'8"
Travis: age 17, brown eyes, brown hair, 6'4"
Mikayla: age 15, green eyes, black hair, 5'6"

Warlocks:
Alfred: age 29, green eyes, brown hair, 6'1"
James: age 10, blue eyes, black hair/silver
  tips, 4'5"
Dwayne: age 22, black eyes, auburn hair,
  5'11"

Witch:
Gala: age 26, black eyes, neon red hair, 4'10"

Genie:
Sylvia: age 20, blue eyes, brown hair/purple
  underneath, 5'5"

Werewolves:
Adam: age 8, brown eyes, brown hair, 5'2"
Tyler: age 16, blue eyes, brown hair, 6'0"
Aaron: age 15, grey eyes, orange hair, 5'9"
Jeff: age 16, brown eyes, blonde hair, 5'10"
Margret: age 13, blue eyes, black hair, 4'9"
John: age 14, green eyes, red hair, 5'0"
Paul: age 16, brown eyes, brown hair, 6'1"
Mr. Watson: age 32, brown eyes, brown/
    balding hair, 7'1"
Lynette: age 12, green eyes, black hair, 5'6"
Sandy: age 12, green eyes, black hair, 5'7"

"Lynette and Sandy are twins. And I said what everyone looked like so we wouldn't get everyone confused. There is a ghost but they won't tell us who they are. So our total is twenty-eight. Do we need more?"

"Wow, you're being really calm about this. Are you suddenly okay with the fact that a bunch of people are risking their lives for us?" Ryan said.

I still wouldn't look at him. I couldn't. The thought of marrying him came back hard when I did. I'd been blocking my thoughts from him ever since Grace had brought it up. At first he was worried, but after a while he just let it go.

"No. I'm not okay with it. What other choice do I have though?" I said, looking down at my awful handwriting.

Suddenly, he was standing over me. He pulled the paper out of my hands and sat on my lap so I had to look at him. He didn't give me much time to react because his lips were on mine.

We sat that way until we heard a knock on my door. At inhuman speed, Ryan was lying on my bed and the list was back in my hands.

"Come in!" Ryan said toward the door.

Good thing too. It would've sounded choked coming from me.

Duke walked in.

"What do we do now," he said as the door closed, "about the fight I mean."

"Well, we have twenty-eight people total. We've got to find a place to meet, and also train. Plus, we don't even know when we are fighting." I told him.

"I'll probably be the one training everyone, I guess." Ryan whispered.

"Why you?"

"You don't know how many fights, supernatural fights, that I've been in. Mostly because of my dad."

"How many?"

"It doesn't matter. But I'm a good fighter. And a good teacher."

"Okay then. You'll teach us."

"Yeah."

"And I'll help you." Duke said.

"Okay, that's cool." Ryan said smiling.

I stared out the window.

"I'm sorry sis." Duke said quietly.

I looked up at him.

"Why?" I asked confused.

"I know you don't want me in the fight and I'm sorry about it. But you're my sister and I have to help protect you."

"Don't worry about it. I'm fine."

"Oh, don't even try lying like that." Ryan said rolling his eyes.

"Well, like you said, it's his choice, not mine. So, yeah, I'm fine."

"I don't know if that's true. Why have you been blocking me out?"

"What do you mean?" I stalled.

"Oh you know very well what I mean. You've been blocking me since we were at your sister's house talking about . . ."

He stopped abruptly. His eyes went blank as he continued to stare at me.

"Ryan?" I said nervously.

At that second, I lost my hold on my thoughts. All the things I had thought of since we were at Grace's house came back. Ryan read it all as it passed through my mind again.

There was a gleam in his eyes when my thoughts caught up to present time. He was still staring at me, his jaw had dropped.

"Ryan?" I said again.

"Hey, man? You okay?" Duke asked moving toward Ryan.

"Yeah, I'm okay," Ryan said, coming back, "Duke, could you step out for a few minutes?"

Duke walked out and shut the door behind himself.

Ryan just stood and stared at me.

"Um . . . Ryan?" I said.

"We're too young." he barely whispered.

"I know, but I didn't mean . . ."

"We can't. I want to too. But we just . . . I just . . . young. We're too young . . . I . . ."

"Now you see why I was blocking you. I didn't mean now . . ."

"That's what you said in your thoughts. But I can't marry you *now.*"

My eyes started to sting. I realized I was getting ready to cry. Rejection. I turned away from him and the tears spilled over and ran down my face.

"Come on. Don't cry." Ryan said in a pained voice.

I heard something shatter and turned to see what had happened. He was shaking glass out of his hair. I looked down at his feet, there was a broken mirror. He looked up at me.

"I'm sorry. I'll get you a new mirror." he said.

"Don't worry about it." I sniffed.

"You're not making this any easier. Why are you crying?"

I shrugged.

"I hurt your feelings!" not a question, a statement of fact. "Oh my God. I'm sorry Ash . . . I just . . ."

He walked over and wrapped his arms around me.

"Tell me what to do? We can't get married *now*! We're too young. They'll all think I knocked you up!" he said almost in tears.

I was hurting him. He wanted it just as much as I did, but he was worried about my reputation.

"We don't have to *now*." I assured him.

"But you want it to be now. So do I . . ."

We just stared into each other's eyes until we were interrupted by another knock on my door. I looked at the door but didn't say anything. Ryan still had his arms around me and was looking at my face when he told whoever it was at the door to come in.

"Hey, Ryan. Your mom called. She wants you to come home now." Duke said.

"Okay. Thanks Duke."

Ryan kissed my forehead then walked out with my brother. I was left alone with my thoughts.

*　　*　　*

"Hey, Ashlee!" one of my new friends yelled down the hall.

Mikayla, one of the vampires that were helping us in the fight, had come early and was staying with my sister. To be inconspicuous she had to attend school.

I turned just as she reached me.

"Hey, Mikayla. Did you need something?" I asked, knowing the answer already.

Mikayla had gone to an academy for vampires only, so she still wasn't used to the weird classes here. Plus, she was still getting lost.

"Yeah. I kind of forgot where the cafeteria is. Again." she answered.

"You just walked out of it. And you don't have lunch until 5th period, this is 3rd period."

"I thought that was the Biology room!"

"No. And you don't have Biology until 7th period."

"Then where am I supposed to be now?"

"You're supposed to be in computers."

"Where's that?"

"The library."

"Where's that?"

I sighed. This was going to be another long day. Like yesterday, the day after Ryan and I had the awkward talk about marriage.

"I'll take you to it." I sighed.

"Thanks! You're the best!" she hugged me.

I walked her to the library. I didn't have to talk much. She did enough talking for the two of us. Rambling on about how she wants to meet the perfect vampire guy and marry him, how I was lucky that I married Ryan. I had to remind her that we were dating and that we weren't married. Ryan would love reading that from my mind.

She left me when I got her to the library, promising that she'd find me at lunch. If she could remember when and where it was.

So now I was left walking to my next class alone. The halls were completely empty. I must be tardy. Who cares? I had to help a vampire find her class. That's called citizenship, or community service or something like that.

Out of nowhere I felt someone following me. Mikayla? No, I just left her and she wouldn't leave the class room until the bell rang. She loved watching the weird humans. I reached out with my mind. When I did I almost froze in mid step and fell.

Jafar! Oh my gosh. She'd gone to the trouble to stalk me at *school* now! That girl had issues.

I sent a message through my thoughts to Ryan. We recently learned we could do this from a distance.

Ryan! Jafar's following me and I'm really scared come help me!

His answer was almost instantaneous:

Hold on Ash. I'll be there in two seconds. She won't do anything to you as long as you're in the building. As long as I'm in the same building.

I counted in my head. One. There was a gush of wind. Two. He was right there in front of me.

Ryan walked up to me and took my hand. With a sharp look at something, or someone, I couldn't see, he started dragging me toward our class.

"I got a text from one of our . . . helpers." he said conversationally.

He pulled out his phone and handed it to me:

HEY, THIS IS STEFAN. I'M PLANNING ON COMING TO YOUR TOWN THIS AFTERNOON.

I SHOULD ATTEND SCHOOL WITH YOU, AS I AM ONLY EIGHTEEN. I WOULD LIKE TO KNOW WHERE TO MEET YOU. IF YOU COULD TEXT ME BACK IT WOULD BE MUCH APPRECIATED.

THANKS ☺

~STEFAN~

"Did you text him back?" I asked handing the phone back.

"Yes. I told him to meet us at your sister's house. Then I texted your sister and told her he was coming there."

"Okay, I guess you have it all under control."

"Did you have any doubt that I did?"

"Of course not. I know you can handle anything."

"Except talking to you about marriage."

Random. I had thought we were done with this. We had agreed that we were too young. Then he had to leave because his mom wanted him home.

"What do you mean?" I asked.

"I could barely make words that were comprehendible. I stuttered a lot. Plus, you did most of the talking anyway." he said.

"Well, we could talk about it later. When we aren't in school, there aren't any cameras, and *she* isn't following us."

"Okay. I promise I'll actually *talk* this time."

"Okay." I laughed.

We were at our classroom door.

"Promise me another thing?" I said to him.

"I'd promise you the world. What is it?"

"Don't get jealous of all the guys that are going to be coming to help us in the fight?"

He chuckled. "I promise, sweetheart."

We walked into the classroom.

*   *   *

"What's this Stefan guy look like? Is he tall? Does he have blue eyes? Does he like short girls? Does he like romantic walks in the moon light? Does he . . . ."

"Mikayla! I already told you! I don't really know anything about him. All I know is he is eighteen, has blue eyes and black hair, and that he's 6'3", plus his name, obviously." I said for the billionth time.

We were walking to Grace's house. Ryan kept laughing and smiling every time I had to repeat myself, which was very often because Mikayla kept asking the same questions over and over again. She'd begged me to ask him to send a picture of himself to my phone, but I saw Ryan tense so I told her we were almost to the house, might as well wait.

She'd finally stopped asking me random questions when the house came into view.

Apparently nobody was in the mood for human speed. Mikayla sped off to the porch, and Ryan picked me up and ran right behind her.

We all walked through the door at the same time.

"GRACE!" I shouted.

"What? I'm in the kitchen." she replied, "I'll be out in a second just sit down in the living room, or should I say the *dead* room." no one laughed.

"You do realize that you have a dry sense of humor?" I sighed, "By the way, where are all the fighters going to stay? Your house isn't that big."

"You don't *think* it's big. Yeah, it's actually huge. Looks very tiny on the outside. It's all an illusion."

"So how many rooms does this thing have?"

"At least thirty, counting my room."

"Cool."

Grace came out of the kitchen. She was carrying a tray of food. Ryan stood and helped her with it.

"Thanks Ryan. Hey, Mikayla. Go put your school stuff in your room, and tell Stefan to come down here." Grace said as Ryan took the tray.

"Okay."

Mikayla grabbed her books and started up the stairs. I looked at Ryan and then heard a loud crash. I jumped up and ran to the stairs.

Mikayla was being helped back to her feet by a tall boy with black hair. Stefan. He stooped back down and grabbed her books for her. When he stood up, that's when he actually saw her.

The look in Stefan's eyes was like the way Ryan looked at me. And Mikayla looked like I did when Ryan climbed through my window every night.

They were instantly in love. I could tell.

"Um . . . Thanks. Stefan?" Mikayla whispered.

"Yes. And you're welcome. Your name is Mikayla, right?"

He had a pretty cute guy voice. No wonder Mikayla trembled. Ryan gave me a sharp look. *Sorry honey!* I thought toward him. He nodded.

"Yes. I'm Mikayla." I heard her answer.

"Were you coming to get me? I'm really sorry."

"Yeah. I was taking my books to my room too."

"I'll take them there, love."

"Um . . . Okay. Thanks."

"No problem. You might want some ice for your head, it's starting to swell."

He looked extremely worried.

"All right. Hey, Grace? Can you get me an ice-pack?"

"I'll get it. C'mon Mikayla." I said grabbing her hand.

Stefan took Mikayla's books and ran upstairs. I dragged Mikayla into the kitchen, got in the freezer and grabbed one of the many ice-packs. I handed it to her and she put it to the lump forming on her forehead.

"You like him." I said. Not a question.

"I mean, I guess. He's really hot. And his voice . . . oh my God! To die for, if I wasn't already dead-ish."

"Well, he really likes you."

"How do you know? Oh my gosh. Did you read his mind Ash? I thought you said you don't like doing that?"

"No. I didn't read his mind. You could tell by the way he acted. I mean, he called you 'love.' Yeah he likes you. A lot."

"Cool. Do you think you could possibly . . . ?"

"Hook you up? Yeah, totally."

"OH MY GOSH! Thank you, thank you, thank you!"

She jumped into my arms. I hugged her back. It's weird, I've only known her for two days and we were already this close. It was better than human friends.

"C'mon. You got to go flirt with the guy that I'm hooking you up with so he knows you like him." I told her.

She smiled at me and we walked out into the *dead* room together.

*   *   *

It had been a long day. Ryan and I walked to the park to spend some time alone. But the park was packed with people, dogs, and Jafar. So we left quickly.

We went to my house and stayed in my room. My brother joined us. Ryan looked at me with wary eyes. Duke flipped my TV on.

"So what are you guys doing?" he said trying to make conversation.

Ryan and I stared at him.

"I came at a bad time, didn't I?"

We nodded in unison.

"Oh, well . . . . Awkward! I'll just leave now."

He got up and walked out, shutting the door behind himself. Ryan grabbed the TV remote and turned it off.

"So, where do you want to start?" I asked quietly.

"Well, we know it can't be now. We're too young. People would think . . . inaccurate things. Plus, our parents would never allow it. Trust me, they would notice." he said rubbing the back of his neck.

"What are we discussing then? Reasons we can't?"

"No. I'm just starting off with that."

"Either way. I have a question for you, and I really hope that you don't take it the wrong way."

I paused. He just kept looking at me.

I continued.

"Do you really want to do this?"

"Of course I do. Why would I be here discussing it if I didn't? Never doubt that I'm madly in love with you."

"Okay. That's all I wanted to know."

"Will this prove it?"

He got down on one knee. Reaching in his pocket he pulled out a jewelry case, the size of a ring case. He opened it and held it out to me. It was a diamond ring. I gasped, bringing my hand to my mouth.

"Ashlee Renee Teaford . . . Will you marry me?" he said, smiling at my shocked face.

"I . . . yes! Absolutely yes! But, when did you get that ring?"

He slipped the ring on my right hand ring finger. Right hand so no one would think anything of it. He got up and wrapped his arms around me, pressing his face into my hair.

"I got the ring the first day I met you. Before I came back through the window." he whispered into my hair.

I smiled. He had liked me that long. He had wanted it longer than I had.

"I'm sorry that the ring isn't on the actual finger. I just don't want it to be obvious. Although your sister will definitely know. As well as Mikayla." he apologized.

"It's okay."

I pulled away from him. Looked him in the eyes as my tears started falling. He took my face in his hands and leaned in.

Then there was a knock at my door.

Ryan dropped his hands, clearly angry with whoever was on the other side of the door.

"What?" he said through his teeth.

My brother peeked in the room.

"Ryan, calm down." I whispered, grabbing his hand and squeezing it.

"Hey, man. Your mom called. She . . ." Duke began.

". . . Wants me home." Ryan finished for him.

"Yeah."

Ryan turned to me. He brought his hand up to my cheek.

"*Te amo.* I love you." he whispered.

He kissed my forehead and walked out of my room with Duke.

When they were gone I stared down at the diamond ring. On the wrong finger, but I didn't want to move it. I wanted Ryan to move it to the left hand when the time came.

I realized that I no longer had a *boyfriend*. I now had a *fiancé*. I liked the sound of it too.

I got up and jumped onto my bed. I fell asleep within seconds.

* * *

That night I had my first nightmare since Ryan had come into my life. They used to happen almost every night before he came to town.

"I never loved you. I've always loved someone else. And you killed her!" Ryan screamed.

"*I didn't know! I thought you loved me? More than your own life? What happened?*" *I cried.*

"*It was never true. I loved her ever since I laid eyes on her. Why would I ever love you? Why would anyone love you?*"

The ghost of Karla floated toward us. She was staring at Ryan; she only had eyes for him. She floated to his side and put an arm around him. He wrapped his arms around her like he had done to me for all those months.

He kissed her on the mouth, like he usually kissed me. To my horror and surprise, he didn't go through her. They could touch, like she wasn't even a ghost.

I ran toward them. As I approached I passed through them as if I was smoke. I looked down. It looked like I was dissolving. A new voice spoke and I looked up.

"*Why aren't you back at the house guys? Alex is going to get mad. Plus, I need help with this stupid mutt.*" *Jafar said.*

On a leash beside her was my brother in wolf-form. He looked like they had been abusing him. I screamed. No one showed any sign that they had heard me. I ran at Jafar and tried to tackle her, but again I passed through her and fell to the ground. I was the ghost now.

I woke up then. I had fallen out of my bed onto the floor. Something grabbed my hand.

"It's okay. It's me." Ryan said soothingly.

I looked up at him. This was real. The other thing had to be a nightmare. Ryan would never join Jafar and Alex. And he loved me, that's why I was wearing the ring. We *both* killed Karla so he couldn't just blame me. Either way, he and Karla had glared at each other and hated each other since they had met.

"What happened? How'd you fall out of bed?" Ryan asked concerned. He was wearing a worried expression.

"Bad dream." I left my thoughts open.

I could tell he was reading them because the look on his face. After he was done he hugged me close to his chest.

"You do know I would never say that to you?" he said. It sounded like he was crying.

"I know."

". . . And I hated Karla. You know that?"

"Yes, I know."

". . . I would never join Alex. You know that too, right?"

"Yes, I do."

". . . I love you. How did you know the 'more than my own life' thing? I've never said that."

"Not out loud."

"You read my mind? When?"

"That night you called Tyler and Aaron."

"I thought you didn't like reading minds?" he said a little smugly.

"The expression you had, it made me. And you wouldn't tell me what was going on with Tyler. You looked annoyed. I had to read your mind. Please don't be mad."

"Ash, I'm not mad. I'm actually glad you read my mind."

"I love you Ryan."

"Love you too Ash. And don't be afraid to read my mind. Okay?"

"Okay. Thanks."

CHAPTER 12
Rejected

I woke up that morning with a vague idea of what had happened that night. The memory of the nightmare already fading, making me unable to remember why I fell asleep with tears in my eyes. Ryan was there when I woke but wouldn't say anything about the dream, probably thinking I didn't want it to be mentioned.

As I was watching Ryan climb down the ladder to go home and change, Duke walked in the room.

"Hey sis. Grace wants us to come over. A little over half the people have showed up." he said as he walked to the window, "You got that Ryan?"

"Yeah. I'll meet you guys there." Ryan answered, out of sight now.

I looked over at Duke.

"What about school?" I asked.

"Grace told mom we were helping her finish moving in. Mom called the schools and told them we wouldn't be there."

"Mom doesn't know what's really going on, does she?"

"Give Grace and me some credit sis; we know what we're doing. I learned from the best." he winked at me.

"Okay. Sorry, I'm so used to being paranoid about stuff like that. It's weird having you and Grace know so much."

"I would have found out anyway. Vampires smell different than humans. You kind of smell like flowers, but every vampire smells like a different flower. You smell like roses, Ryan smells like Japanese honey sickle, Grace smells like lilacs, and I don't really recognize what Mikayla smells like. But either way, I would have noticed."

"Okay you would've noticed because I smell weird and Grace would've noticed because she's a vampire too. So I see your point."

"We got to get to Grace's house, come on sis."

"Right. Let's go meet the people who are risking their lives because Ryan doesn't want to run." I said angrily.

"You know why he doesn't want to run. He said it would just give you away to the police, and then you would have Alex *and* the police after you."

My little brother acting as the voice of reason and me being unreasonable. Felt like we switched places.

"I know Duke. Let's go to Grace's."

We walked out the door and Duke shut it behind us. I saw the school bus at the end of the street. And with vampire vision, I saw Jafar at the back window, nails digging into the glass with an angry expression as she looked back at me. Little prep can't follow me now without blowing it; she thought I was going to school today. Seeing me in pajama pants and a tank top really made her day turn around.

I took my brother under my arm, which was hard because he was almost my height now. Five more weeks and he'd be taller than me, all because he's a werewolf. But after those five weeks he will be done growing.

We walked all the way to Grace's house in two minutes. Sometimes it helps having supernatural speed. When we got there we didn't bother knocking and we walked on in to the living room. Nobody was there but Grace and Ryan.

"Hey guys, I was waiting for you to get here before I called them down. You ready?" Grace started talking before we were in the room.

"Yeah, call them down." I heard a voice say, and it took me a second to realize it was me.

"Alright. Come down guys!" she didn't even yell.

There was just Ryan, Grace, Duke, and me. I blinked. I was surrounded by supernatural creatures.

"Whoa." that was all I could say.

Ryan squeezed his way over to me. When he got close enough he grabbed my hand. I looked up at him; his expression was hard to read. So I did what he told me to, I reached out with my mind. He knew I would, and as soon as I did he started talking to me. I couldn't catch all of it.

. . . . *they don't need to be thinking that, and you could have at least changed out of your pajamas.* Ryan thought to me.

I'm sorry, I didn't hear the beginning. Start over? I said confused.

I said, I don't like how they keep staring at you, and if you read their thoughts you'd understand why. They shouldn't be thinking about you like that, because that's reserved for me only, and you could have changed your clothes, because I'm not the only one who likes it.

I don't get it. What are they thinking?

Why don't you read their minds and find out? I don't really want to talk about it.

Could you tell me what is reserved only for you?

You. Your love. Your life. Your arms. Your lips. Everything.

Oh, well yeah. All that is yours.

I know. But it bothers me that they think you might leave me for them, because I'm pretty sure they know we are dating by now. They're mostly vampires, they can read minds.

But remember what Grace said, she can't read minds, and none of her friends can either.

True. But some of these guys might. Be quiet for a second.

We were both quiet. As was everything else in our minds. I could only hear people talking outside my head. Duke had went to mingle and Mikayla was talking to Stefan, but a few guys were still staring at me. Ryan wasn't holding my hand anymore so felt for it but only found his leg; he gave me his hand, knowing that's what I wanted.

Okay, I heard one of them thinking, "I wonder if that hot vamp is dating anyone," and heard another one thinking, "Are those two vamps dating? Probably won't be after the girl meets me." So I'm assuming they can't read minds.

Which leads to the question, "Are we the only ones who can?" and by the way, don't let them bother you. When I look at them, all I see are people, but in a kind of way where I can't see their faces. Because I can only think of your face. Because I'm in love with you, not them. And you know that.

Yeah, I know that.

I stood on my toes and leaned toward him. He knew what I wanted and he gave it to me. He kissed me on the lips passionately; not needing to breathe much makes it unable to tell how long this would go uninterrupted. But, as always, we *were* interrupted. By Mikayla.

"Guys. I know you're in love and all, and that's amazing and everything. But don't you think you should be meeting everyone instead of making out in the corner of the room?" she said without adding punctuation.

"No." Ryan answered, and he kissed the corner of my mouth.

"Yes, we should but . . ." I began.

I stopped short; Ryan had begun to nibble on my bottom lip. I froze. That was more than I was used to in public.

"I get it. Why don't you guys go to my room? It will be more private, and then you can meet everyone."

She walked over to Stefan.

Ryan picked me up and walked up the stairs at human speed, which is odd for him. When we got to the top I looked down the hallway. There was at least thirty rooms, how was Ryan supposed to know which was Mikayla's?

He went to the first door and opened it with his foot. He walked in and shut the door behind him. I looked around; this was obviously Mikayla's room. She had painted it all the colors you could think of, it was as if you were inside a rainbow. Her carpet was multiple colors like the walls. Her bed, her desk, her laptop, everything, as colorful as the walls. She had even painted the ceiling and door.

Ryan walked over to the bed and laid me down, and then he crawled onto the bed beside me. I rolled onto my side so I could see him, and I found him already on his side staring at me.

He wrapped his arms around me and I scooted closer. He looked down at my arms and sat up.

"What are you doing, Ryan?" I asked as he grabbed his shirt collar.

He pulled the T-shirt over his head and handed it to me.

"What?" I asked confused.

"Look at your arms."

I did. There were goose bumps all over my arms. I just realized that Mikayla's room was freezing. I shivered and pulled on Ryan's T-shirt.

"Thanks." I whispered.

He put his hand under my chin and lifted my face closer to his. He leaned in and kissed me.

Next thing I knew we were both laying down, heads on Mikayla's pillow. Then Ryan rolled onto his back, pulling me onto his stomach. Not once breaking the kiss. He took one of his hands out of my hair and moved it to my thigh. His hand kept moving until it reached the bend of my knee. He grabbed my knee and hitched it on his hip then moved his hand to my hip.

I heard voices down stairs.

"Mikayla, have you seen Ryan and Ashlee?" I heard my sister ask.

I heard Mikayla say, "Yes, they went to my room. They'll be back down when they're ready."

My sister's concerned voice interrupted.

"They're *alone* in your room?"

"Yes, I thought they would like some privacy."

Oh yes, I did like the privacy. I could feel Ryan chuckle under me. He pushed me onto my back and was holding himself up above me but he made sure we were still touching; just I didn't feel any of his weight.

He liked the privacy too. He was showing me that. I could tell he'd forgotten about all the guys down stairs. But he was also listening for my sister to come up the stairs.

He moved his mouth to my neck and I turned my head. I was looking for a TV we could turn on if my sister came up here. I found it in the corner of the room, as colorful as everything else. I could probably get up fast enough to turn it on if I had enough of a warning.

Ryan laughed again and his breath tickled my neck.

"Don't worry." he whispered hoarsely.

I lifted his head as he went for my neck again. He smiled and kissed me. I wrapped my arms around his neck and he let some of his weight push down. Then I heard voices again.

"Mikayla! Why would you let them have their privacy? They are teenagers that are in love!" I heard my sister say.

They were in the kitchen away from everyone else.

"That's exactly why I did it." Mikayla explained.

Thank you Mikayla. At least someone gets it.

I vaguely felt Ryan's wandering hands as I heard what my sister said next.

"That's why you *don't* give them privacy! I have to go up there and get them."

I heard the kitchen door open and close and Grace making her way across the living room.

Ryan continued to kiss me as if nothing was happening. I reached under him and pushed on his chest. He moved to my neck again.

I heard my sister on the stairs. How long would it take her to get up here?

"Ryan?" I whispered. My voice sounded as hoarse as his had.

"Mmm?" he answered.

"Grace is coming up the stairs *right this second.*"

"Dang it!"

And he wasn't there. I sat up and saw him turn the TV on. He ran to the door and put his hand on the light switch, looked at me, and I closed my eyes. My eyelids changed from black to red and I opened my eyes. The colors made the room extremely bright. Ryan walked over to me with Mikayla's jacket. I took his shirt off and handed it to him. He threw it on and helped me put the jacket on.

I heard Grace reach the door as he zipped the jacket. He flung himself across the room and landed in a colorful beanbag chair. We both turned toward the TV and pretended to be watching *House of Anubis.*

My sister threw the door open and ran inside.

"You guys better . . ."

She stopped, staring at the TV. Then looking at how much space we had left between us. We were half way across the room from each other and were now staring at Grace. Please let her buy it, PLEASE!

"You guys just came up here to watch TV?" she asked.

"Well, yeah. It was too crowded down there. I get claustrophobic and Ashlee wanted to come with me to make sure I was okay." he wasn't hoarse anymore.

"Oh, I'm sorry. I feel that I was kind of rude and accusing."

"It's okay." Ryan can get out of anything, except when he is dealing with me because I know all of his tricks.

"Could you guys come down to the living room and meet everyone now?"

"Yeah, I'm all better now." he stood and walked over to me, "Come on, Ash. Let's go."

He held out his hand and I took it.

Grace led us back to the living room, where everyone watched us return. Duke ran up to Ryan.

"Dude, you got to meet the genie, she is insanely hot!"

"Excuse me?" I said, eye brows raised.

"Umm, I meant insanely nice," he looked at Ryan, "You have to meet her bro."

"Why does he . . . wait, did you just call him bro?"

"Yeah. Why?"

"Why'd you call him bro?"

"He's close enough to that, might as well refer to him as brother, or bro."

I looked at Ryan. Closer to a brother than even Duke thinks.

"Yeah, I feel the same way kid. But I don't really want to meet the genie right now, okay?" Ryan said, getting out of another thing he didn't want to do.

Although this time he didn't want to go because of me, he didn't want me to be offended.

"Ryan. Ashlee. Could you two come to the kitchen?" Grace asked, I had forgotten she was there. "I need to talk to you guys."

She grabbed Mikayla, who was talking to Stefan, and pulled her into the kitchen. Ryan and I followed.

Grace hopped up on the counter, Mikayla sat down in the middle of the floor, and Ryan sat in one of the kitchen chairs. I walked toward him and he opened his arms. I sat on his lap and looked at Grace. I noticed her and Mikayla were staring at me. Or maybe Ryan and me.

"What?" I asked.

"What is going on?" Grace forced herself to say.

"What do you mean?"

"Mikayla? Mind helping me?"

"No problem." she straightened up.

I leaned back onto Ryan's chest; he put his arms around me and locked his fingers across my stomach.

Mikayla and Grace both looked down at his hands.

"You guys are acting weird," Grace said. "Even Mikayla sees it and she hasn't been here that long."

"Yeah." Mikayla agreed.

"Weird how?" I asked, eyes narrowing.

"You two have been more open around everyone. Making out in the corner of the room as if you were alone. What you're doing now. It's like you are oblivious to the fact that you used to just hold hands in front of us. And now Ryan's so out of it he's kissing your neck while I'm talking."

Ryan pulled away blushing.

"I wasn't out of it. I just . . ."

"Just what? And you guys looked all nervous when Duke called Ryan bro. That was just weird. I don't see how that would . . . Ashlee? Where'd you get that ring?"

I had lifted my right hand to scratch my nose. Her gaze locked on the ring, she repeated her question.

Ryan and I looked at each other wide eyed. Then we shifted our gaze back to her.

"You guys aren't 'dating' anymore, are you?" she asked because of our expressions.

Neither of us answered. Which was answer enough for her.

"So when is it?" Grace asked.

Mikayla looked over at her with an odd expression.

"When's what?" Mikayla asked her.

"Their wedding."

"Wedding!?"

"Yes. Wedding. Do you not listen?"

"I heard you talking about a ring then you asked when it was."

"Wouldn't you be able to put the two together?"

"Well what if you changed subjects? I was barely listening so it's a possibility."

"Okay Mikayla." she turned back to us, "So . . . When is it?"

Ryan and I looked at each other again. We looked back at Mikayla and Grace; they were looking at us expectantly.

"We don't know." I said.

Grace and Mikayla looked at each other. They looked shocked and also hopeful.

"You guys have to talk to her about that. She might not, knowing her. We don't know when because we have to do it after we finish school." Ryan growled.

We looked at him.

"Ask me what?" I said.

"If we can plan your wedding?" Mikayla answered quietly.

"Oh. I was just going to plan with Ryan. You know, to surprise everyone. Plus, it's going to be small anyway."

"Aw. We can't help at all?"

"We won't really need it since it'll be small."

"I told you." Ryan whispered.

"By the way, I need to talk to you." I whispered to him.

"What did I do?"

"Nothing. It's about what we've been discussing."

"The fight?"

"Really?"

"I know you're talking about the wedding, I was joking."

"Ryan that is *not* the type of thing you joke about with a girl." Grace told him.

I stood and so did Ryan. I was hoping we could leave. Ryan had met everyone through mind reading and I could do the same through his. And we had things to discuss.

"We're going to leave." I told Grace.

She looked up at me.

"You haven't even met anyone."

"Ryan has."

"No, he's been out of the room with you."

"Mind reading Grace. Ryan met everyone through it. I'll meet them through his thoughts."

"Oh. Alright. Tell Duke you're leaving, but he doesn't have to go yet if he doesn't want to."

I walked out the kitchen door with Ryan right behind me. Duke was on the other side of the room with Stefan. We walked over to him.

"Hey Ashlee." Stefan greeted, "Hey Ryan."

"Hi Stefan. Duke, Ryan and I are going to leave, but Grace said you didn't have to leave with us." I said.

"Okay sis. I'm going to stay. I want to go talk to your werewolf teacher, Mr. Watson." he walked away.

"Ryan, you go wait in your car."

"How'd you know I took my car?" he looked down at me.

"Ryan. Just go."

"Yes ma'am."

He went out the door. I waited a few seconds then heard the engine start. I looked back at Stefan.

"Did you want to talk to me? Well that is obvious; otherwise you would be with Ryan." Stefan evaluated.

"Yeah. I wanted to know if you like Mikayla."

"Yes. She's a very nice vampire. I haven't found many of those."

"You do realize I'm talking about more than just a friend?"

"Oh . . . Um. I-I guess. Like I said she is very nice. I suppose I do like her that way."

He rubbed the back of his neck.

"Would you like to date her?" I asked.

"Well, yeah. Why?"

"Okay. You're dating her now."

"What?"

"She likes you. You should ask her out."

"Um. Thanks!"

"I have to go before Ryan throws a fit."

I walked out of the house and found Ryan's car parked straight in front of me. He was leaning against the passenger side. When I walked up he opened the door for me. I stopped behind the door.

"Well, I took care of that." I said happily.

"Yeah you did. And I wasn't going to throw a fit."

I laughed. He kissed me on the cheek.

"Get in." he laughed.

I did. He shut the door and got in the car. He headed toward the city limits.

*　　*　　*

We stopped beside Blackies Lake. Ryan led me out to a very narrow path right beside the water. He kept reaching back and helping me when I almost fell into the lake. Too many people have died in that lake and I didn't really fancy joining them.

Finally, we reached the end of the path and it opened up into a cute, little meadow with a giant rock at the other side, opposite from where we were standing. I looked toward the lake; you could see it between two trees that twisted together. It was really pretty when you looked at the lake that way; otherwise it looks horrible and scary.

I started walking toward the rock then stopped short at a scent that I almost didn't catch. I looked back at Ryan. He smelled it too; a werewolf. Not one that we had met either.

Ryan grabbed my hand and pulled me behind him. He crouched in front of me and searched the woods around us with mind, sight, and hearing. We both heard a faint chuckle that a human would never hear, our heads snapped to the right side of the rock. He wasn't out in a human's plain sight yet but Ryan and I could see a silhouette walking toward us.

The guy was roughly six feet tall and looked muscular. I could also see that he had short hair which is normal for people in a small town like mine

He started talking before he entered the clearing.

"Don't worry, sport. I'm not here to try to take your mate. But I am here to help you." his voice was deep.

"With what?" Ryan spat through his teeth.

I looked down at him, then back at the silhouette.

"Well, if you must know little vamp, my father sent me." the dark figure said.

Ryan froze.

"You're Mr. Watson's son?" he whispered.

"How'd you know?" the werewolf said, sincerely surprised.

"I was guessing. You just confirmed it though."

Ryan had obviously heard it in the werewolf's mind. And obviously didn't trust him enough yet to tell him we can read minds. Another thing was, if Mr. Watson had told his son to help us did that mean the dude was helping with the fight?

Ryan nodded. Question answered. Yes.

Mr. Watson's son walked into the clearing. The blazing sun glancing off of his skin. He was covered in sweat, his hair dripping with it. He looked like he'd been chasing our car.

Ryan looked at me out of the corner of his eye. He *had* chased our car.

"My name is Charles. But everyone calls me Char, you can too if you want." Watson's son said.

"Ryan." Ryan said pointing at himself, "Ashlee." pointing at me. Then he was silent.

"Nice to meet you. Could you get up out of that crouch now?"

"I don't know yet."

Char looked offended. I poked Ryan's back.

"Ryan. Stand up." I said.

He hesitated.

"Ryan. Now."

He straightened and put his arm around my shoulders.

"Trained him well I see." Char said.

I glared at him. He took a step back.

"I was kidding." he said looking away.

"It wasn't funny. You must have a dry sense of humor." I snapped.

I grabbed Ryan's hand, the one hanging beside my shoulder.

"I'm sorry." Char whispered.

"Are you here to tell us you're helping with the fight or what?" Ryan asked then put his face in my hair.

"Um, yeah. That is why I'm here. How'd you figure that?"

"Because that's the only thing your father would have you help us with. That's the only thing we *need* help with."

"Oh. I thought you talked to him or something. Since you already knew everything I was going to tell you."

"Can you hurry? We were getting ready to hunt."

"Oh. I'm sorry. You know what I was going to say so I guess I don't need to say it. I'll leave now. You read my mind, so you have my cell phone number." Ryan nodded, "Good-bye."

He turned on his heel and sprinted into the woods that he came from. We waited until we couldn't hear him anymore.

"Are we really going hunting?" I asked, as I did my stomach growled.

Ryan looked down at it then gently put his hand on it.

"Yeah. You're hungry. We are hunting." he answered.

* * *

I was perched in a tree above a rabbit caught in the undergrowth. It knew I was there which was why it was struggling to get free. I jumped down, untangled the rabbit's legs from the vines, brought it up to my chest and just held it there. It started to relax. I walked over to a bush and set it down. It looked up at me quickly, confused, and then it hopped away.

I walked over to Ryan.

"That's the fifth one you've let go. What's up? You have to drink something." he whispered.

I walked into his arms.

"Why won't you drink any of them?" his voice was strained.

"I feel sorry for them. They have a long life ahead of them."

"What if I find you an animal that's dying? Would you drink it? For me?"

"I guess. It has to be naturally dying. Not you almost killing it and then giving it to me."

"Okay. I'll find something. Wait here and I'll yell if I find anything. You can decide if you want it or not."

He was gone in the blink of an eye. I could still hear him running through the woods nearby.

"Ashlee! Found something!" Ryan yelled.

I ran in the direction of his voice. I broke through the trees and found myself in another clearing. Ryan was standing in the middle of it. I looked around for a dying animal. There was nothing. All of a sudden the woods had gotten quiet.

"Ryan," I said slowly, "there's no dying animal here."

"I know my dear." he answered.

It was Ryan's voice, but it was a little bit . . . off. All of my vampire instincts told me to turn around and run.

The guy standing there, in the middle of the clearing, looked and talked a little like my boyfriend (or fiancé, whichever), but something was wrong.

Ryan didn't call me 'my dear' or psych me out like this guy had. In fact, Ryan wasn't that tall and he didn't have tiny, almost invisible, streaks of brown in his hair. And Ryan most certainly did not have iridescent purple eyes.

When I saw the eyes they were so familiar. Jafar had that same color and I'm pretty sure Alexander did too. My heart skipped a beat.

Alexander.

He was exactly that tall. He had hair the color of the semi-invisible streaks. A little bit of his voice had leaked into Ryan's.

Alexander had lured me there by pretending to be Ryan.

"Hello, Alexander." I said sharply.

He frowned.

"How'd you recognize me? I mean, I expected you to realize it wasn't your boyfriend. I didn't think you'd know me."

"I remember you from my past."

"But that was long ago. I kept my face hidden in the shadows and you were unconscious. I told you my name and that was all."

"I wasn't talking about the night you changed me, although, I remember that perfectly. Your baseball bat didn't *completely* knock me out."

"Yes, you *were* a very strong human. Stronger than I had expected. You put up a good fight."

"My dad had started teaching me to defend myself the day I started walking."

"I could image why. The man's a werewolf, is he not?"

I didn't answer. I kept my mouth shut in a tight line.

"Ashlee!" I heard Ryan's panicked scream.

Alexander and I both looked toward the noise. Alexander morphed back to his own appearance.

"I must go now," Alexander began. "But I would like to ask you and your boyfriend to join me and my army. I'm sure you will think about the offer and say-"

"No." I said flatly.

"I beg your pardon?"

"I said no. Now get out of here before Ryan gets here."

Alexander glared at me. For a second I thought he was going to attack me.

"You will regret your decision, little girl. Don't think I won't have my army destroy you and Ryan. I bid thee farewell. But heed my warning." he spat every word through his teeth.

Alexander turned on his heel and disappeared into thin air. Or that's what it looked like. He had actually turned into a bat and flew toward my face. He got swatted out of the air before he reached me.

I looked over and saw Ryan glaring down at the bat. He looked up at me.

"Is that the only reason you yelled for help? Because of a stupid bat?" he said.

"I didn't yell for help, Ryan."

"But I heard you . . ."

I pointed to the bat at his feet.

"Don't tell me that *bat* yelled in your voice." he said sharply.

"That's not just a bat, Ryan, it's Alexander."

He looked down at the bat again. Apparently he saw the resemblance, because he stomped his foot down on the bat as it tried to get up. I heard tiny bones cracking. Ryan lifted his foot and I saw the bat's wings twitching.

"Come on," Ryan said grabbing my hand and pulling me away. "Back to the car. We are done hunting."

I didn't argue. We made it to the car within seconds. As we were leaving, I saw Alexander at the tree line watching us leave. His nose was broken but already healing. All his other bones had already been healed. The look in his eyes was pure loathing.

"Step on it!" I told Ryan.

He looked in the rearview mirror and put the gas pedal all the way to the floor.

*   *   *

"I think it's time I introduce you to some people. We are stopping at your sister's place first though. We have to warn them, the fight may be sooner than we anticipated." Ryan told me as we hit the city limits.

"Alright." I said in a choked voice.

Ryan glanced at me nervously. He reached over and took my hand, pulling my arm toward him. He rested our intertwined hands on his thigh and absently stroked my hand with his thumb.

I stared out the window. We were already on Grace's street because Ryan still had the pedal to the floor.

As if that thought had reminded him, he let off the gas and started to ease on the brake.

He stopped the car directly in front of Grace's house, right behind her Mustang.

We both jumped out of the car as soon as it stopped and ran to the door at vampire speed. I only knocked once when some boy answered the door.

"Hello. I'm James. State your names and business." the boy sounded as if he had said this line more than he wanted to.

"Ashlee and Ryan. We are here to see my sister, Grace." I announced.

James's eyes widened. "It's almost time?"

"Yes. We just told him no."

James looked down the street both ways and then stood aside so we could enter.

I walked straight through the living room, which was now packed with supernatural creatures, and I kept going until I shoved my way into the kitchen. Ryan was right behind me.

"Grace," I said staring at her. "We need to talk."

She looked up and saw the look on my face. Her eyes widened in fear, like James's, but she just nodded.

I explained to her what had happened, including the part about Char. I could tell Ryan still didn't like Char, even though he was going to help us.

"So, wait. You're telling me that you, straight up, told him no, then he threatened your life?" Grace asked me, again.

I nodded.

"That's it. We need to start training. Now. I'm going to kill the man myself. Nobody threatens my little sister. *NOBODY!*"

"I'll start the training as soon as we get back. Where is Duke?" Ryan told her.

She pointed to the corner of the kitchen. Duke was curled up in a ball on the floor; it looked like he was sleeping. When Ryan said his name his head snapped up. He saw us, jumped to his feet, and walked over and sat on my lap.

"What's going on?" he asked.

"I could ask you the same thing," Ryan looked worried. "Why were you on the floor?"

"It felt like I was Changing, so Grace brought me in here away from everyone else."

"Did you Change?" I asked.

"No, it was just a stomach ache from Grace's cooking."

Grace smiled sheepishly. "My cooking isn't the best."

We laughed.

"So, what did you need me for?" Duke asked, looking at Ryan.

"We are going for a ride."

"Cool. Where to, bro?"

"My house. I'm introducing you to my family. I figure it's about time now."

Duke and I looked at each other. Duke stood and patted Ryan on the back. Ryan looked up and smiled at him.

"Ryan, as long as your parents like me, I'm fine." I told him.

"You're afraid they won't like you and make us break up?" he actually laughed at this.

"Yes. Why are you laughing?"

"Ashlee. They know I'm happy. They aren't going to mess that up. Don't worry about making them like you. Although, them liking you is a bonus."

"Okay. Before we go, do you have any siblings? Or any other family member we should know about?"

His face went dark. There was sadness in his eyes.

"I have a brother. But you'll just have to understand. He's . . . different."

"Ryan, it's probably not that . . ."

"You don't get it. Come on. You have to see it to understand."

He turned and left the kitchen. Duke and I exchanged looks and then followed Ryan to the car.

CHAPTER 13

Prodigy

We pulled into Ryan's driveway. I saw one other car and that was it. They must share that one.

"They're all here, and they know we are here." Ryan announced.

"Okay. Any warnings?" I asked.

"Yeah. Just one. Don't make fun of my brother."

"Why would we make fun of him?"

"You'll see. And try not to stare."

"Okay."

I got out of the car. My knees were shaking so bad I almost fell. Ryan was there as soon as my door was shut. He put an arm around my waist so I wouldn't fall.

Duke was already out of the car and waiting for us. We all walked to the door together.

Ryan opened the door and dragged me in behind him. I grabbed Duke's hand and pulled him along with me. He rubbed his thumb in a circle on my hand, trying to comfort me. I looked back and he smiled. He wasn't nervous at all; then again he wasn't Ryan's girlfriend.

Fiancée. Ryan corrected in my mind.

Yeah. I know.

You don't need to be nervous. He laughed.

We walked into something that resembled a family room. The only thing was that it didn't look like a normal family room. You could tell these people weren't human. Battle armor was hanging on two of the four walls. On the other two walls were paintings of death scenes. Most of the paintings were so gruesome that I wanted to cover Duke's eyes.

Across the room there was a wraparound sofa. Three people were sitting on it spaced at least five feet apart, as if they couldn't stand to be near each other.

The person closest to us was a woman. Ryan's mom. She was pretty. She had Ryan's hair or, I guess I should say: he had hers. She had bright green eyes. And I mean *bright* green. It's probably because the werewolf thing. She also had the scars on her from the attack. The scars were pretty thick too.

The next person was a man. I believe he was Ryan's father. He looked too old to be a brother. He had black hair and piercing red eyes that kind of scared me. He had some stubble on his chin. The casual type of stubble that says: 'oh, I guess I forgot to shave this morning' or something. He had a little bit of dried blood on his chin. I tried not to think of who it came from.

The last person was a boy. He looked normal, which made me wonder what Ryan was going on about. The boy had blue eyes and blonde hair. If he was standing he'd probably be at least 5'11". He looked almost exactly like Ryan, only taller. I wondered why he never went to school.

"Hi, mom. Dad. Cole." Ryan said.

They nodded.

"This is Ashlee. My girlfriend," he gestured toward me, "and this is her brother, Adam. He goes by Duke."

There was a murmur of what I thought were greetings.

Cole stood and crossed the room. He held out his hand to me. We shook hands then he shook hands with my brother.

"It's very nice to meet you." he said.

I flinched. He sounded exactly like Ryan. I looked at Ryan out of the corner of my eye.

"Cole is my twin brother." he explained to me.

That made sense.

Cole's head snapped to the right.

"What?" he asked.

He was looking at nothing.

"No. I don't think so. I'm very sorry." he said to no one.

Everyone was watching him.

"I'm very sorry. Would you like me to help you cross over?"

A pause.

"Okay. I get it. Good-bye."

He looked back at me. I realized only Duke and I were still watching him.

I mumbled an apology.

"It's okay Ashlee. I know you didn't understand that. See, I am a necromancer." he said, trying to explain.

"A what?" I said stupidly.

"A necromancer," he smiled at me. "A person who can communicate with ghosts. See, supernaturals like you can only see tiny shimmers of ghosts. I see them as if they were actual people."

"Oh."

I looked up at Ryan.

"So, mom." he said to change the subject, "what are we having for dinner?"

"Steak. Does your girlfriend like it raw?"

"Just fix it how you usually do for me."

I looked at him funny.

"Mom fixes ours rare. But Cole's is usually well done. He's the only one who doesn't like blood." Ryan explained to me.

"I'd like mine done the same as Cole's please." Duke said, speaking for the first time.

"Of course, sweetie. But you're a werewolf; wouldn't you prefer the bloodiest you can get?" Ryan's mother said.

"Um . . . no thanks. I'd rather have it well done."

"Suit yourself."

She turned and walked into what I guessed was the kitchen. Ryan turned to his father and pointed to his chin. Ryan's dad lifted a hand to his face and, apparently, found the dried blood.

"Um. I'm going to go wash up before dinner." he got up and walked down a hallway.

"So . . . want to see Cole's and my room?" Ryan asked me.

"Sure."

"Okay. Come on, Cole."

Cole smiled and followed us, walking beside my brother.

*   *   *

We all sat around the dining room table. Ryan's mom was about to bring the steaks in. I offered to help but she said to just sit down and not worry about it.

Ryan had shown Duke and me his and Cole's room. It wasn't anything special. But it was interesting. It was like it had been cut in half. Ryan's half of the room had two swords and a shield hanging on the wall. The walls were painted red. It was neatly organized and everything in order. He also had a bookshelf full of books and also a random dagger.

Cole's half of the room was completely opposite. Instead of swords, daggers, and shields, there were print-outs of random statistics and pictures pinned all over the walls. His walls were painted like the color wheel. There was a desk with opened books on it, and books were strung across the floor and bed.

I asked Cole about school because of all the books. He had handed me a book off his desk. It was in a different language. He explained to me that he was 'home schooled' in necromancy.

Then Ryan's mom had told us to come in the dining room for dinner.

Ryan's mom walked through the door with six plates in one hand and six drinks in the other. She sat them all down in front of who they belonged to.

I looked at the steak in front of me. Blood was still oozing out of it. I looked at Ryan. He had cut his steak into cubes. As I watched he picked up a cube with his fork, brought it to his mouth, and then sunk his teeth into it. When he had sucked all the blood out, he dropped the shriveled piece of meat to the plate and picked up another cube.

I did the same with mine. Surprisingly, it tasted amazing. I didn't realize how thirsty I was until the blood was slithering down my throat. I finished the whole steak within three minutes.

Ryan looked up and laughed. He was only half way done with his. I looked around. Everyone else still had at least half a steak on their plate. I felt my face get hot as everyone stared at me.

"Ryan, don't laugh at her," Ryan's mom defended me. "She was just thirsty. She probably hasn't fed for days."

Ryan looked over at me.

"When *was* the last time you fed?" he asked me.

"I don't know. About a month ago." my voice sounded weird because my fangs were still elongated.

I retracted them.

"Would you like more, honey?" Ryan's mom asked.

"No, thanks. I'm full now." I said, voice normal again.

"Well, if you want you can go watch TV in the other room."

"Okay. Thank you."

I got up and went to the family room. I picked a soft spot on the sofa. The softest spot was the wedge in the corner. I curled up there and turned the TV on to a random show. Something on Nickelodeon. I didn't watch it. I closed my eyes.

*   *   *

"Hey, Ashlee," Ryan said. "Wake up."

I rubbed my eyes and sat up blinking. I looked around for Ryan. I only found Cole. Then I realized it was him who had spoken.

"You look disoriented." he said smiling.

"Little bit. I thought you were Ryan."

"Because we sound the same?"

"Yeah."

"Mom gets confused by that too. Don't worry."

I smiled and looked at the TV. He'd changed the channel and was watching *Ghost Adventures* now. I looked at him with an eyebrow raised. He laughed.

"I like to watch it because of the people." he explained.

"What about the people?"

"It's funny because they are humans."

"And . . ."

"You know supernaturals can see shimmers?"

"Yeah?"

"Humans can't see anything."

"Oh."

We watched TV in silence for the rest of the show. I found out why he thought it was funny. The people on the show seemed schizophrenic to me. I never saw the 'ghosts' they were talking about, and everything looked *so* fake. We even laughed a few times.

When the show was over Ryan came in and sat beside me. He draped his arm around my shoulders and I laid my head on his arm.

"What are you guys watching?" Ryan asked.

"We were watching *Ghost Adventures* but it's over now." I answered.

Cole picked up the remote and flipped through the guide. He paused suddenly and looked to his right. I followed his gaze. I saw what looked like a shimmer of silver.

A ghost.

"Hello." Cole said.

A pause.

"I haven't. Don't worry." he muttered.

He looked back at the TV and flipped through the guide again as the shimmer disappeared. I looked away from him.

"That's the ghost who's helping in the fight." Cole frowned.

"Oh. Who is it?" Ryan asked.

"I'm not allowed to say. I promised."

He was still frowning.

"What's wrong, Cole?" I asked.

"What do you mean?" he looked surprised.

"You're frowning."

"Oh. That's only because Ryan won't let me help you guys."

I looked at Ryan. He was staring out the window. My brother was allowed to risk his life but Cole wasn't?

"You don't get it Ashlee." Ryan answered my thoughts.

He was still staring out the window.

"How is that fair?" I said through my teeth.

He looked at me then. "Ashlee. Cole is more human than Duke."

"So?"

"Cole is easier to kill."

"I think he'd be smart enough not to get himself killed."

"I don't want to risk it."

"Well, send him with some battle armor."

I pointed to it on the wall.

"No." he said in a strained voice.

"Remember what you said about Duke? It's his choice."

Ryan looked guilty. He remembered. I looked at Cole.

"Would you like to fight?" I asked.

"Yes, please." he answered shyly.

"You're in. We are starting training tomorrow. Just come with Ryan."

I looked up at the clock. It was eight thirty.

"It's late. Where is Duke?" I said.

"Talking to my mom. I'll go save him." Ryan answered and left the room.

"Thanks for letting me help." Cole whispered to me.

"No problem."

Ryan walked through the kitchen door with a relieved looking Duke.

"Come on. I'll walk you guys home." he said.

Cole and I stood and followed him and Duke to the door. Cole pulled Ryan to the side. They had a whispered conversation that looked like an argument. I couldn't hear what they were arguing about though. They walked back over to us.

"Let's go." Ryan said opening the door.

Cole walked out the door first. Then Duke and me. Ryan walked out last and shut the door behind him.

We walked away from the car which told me that Ryan wasn't going home before morning. I suppose Cole was going to walk home, seeing as Ryan wasn't going to supply a ride.

When we got to the end of my street Ryan tackled me into a bush. Duke and Cole dived in behind us.

"Dude, was that Jafar and Alexander?" Duke asked.

"Yeah, they're waiting for us. We have to go to Grace's" Ryan whispered.

We sneaked out of the bush and ran to Grace's. It was slower having Cole there. I didn't like it much, but I tolerated it.

Once or twice I saw a few shimmers of ghosts beside Cole. He ignored all of them. They disappeared when they figured out that he wasn't listening. I'd have to remember to ask him why they all swarmed to him and no one else.

Ryan was reading my thoughts.

"It's because they sense that he can see, hear, and interact with them. They always have something to say and they'll say it to anyone who can hear them." he answered.

Cole looked at him funny but didn't say anything, just kept running.

We finally got to Grace's house. It seemed like it had taken forever. I looked behind us thinking that Jafar and Alex probably would have caught up. All that I saw was an empty street.

We ran up the steps and busted through Grace's front door. There were more supernaturals than last time. It looked like everyone had shown up now. Even some of the people that lived in town were here.

Grace ran up to us. She started checking me to see if I was okay. Then she went down the line and check Ryan and Duke. When she got to Cole she paused.

"I already checked you." she said confused.

"No. I'm not Ryan. I'm Cole, his twin." Cole told her.

She looked between the two of them then shook her head.

"Okay. Are you all okay though? Dad called and said that there were two vampires outside your house."

"We're okay. Wait . . . Did you say *dad* told you?" I said.

"Yes. Dad. You do realize that if he's a werewolf he *knows* you're a vampire. And Ryan and me. How do you think Alex hasn't found you all these years? Dad has been protecting you. He told me on the phone."

"Yeah. That makes sense now."

"So you guys will have to stay here."

"What about Ryan's house?"

"Alexander has people stationed there too. Everyone is here. Every single person on your list. I don't know if the ghost is here though."

"Yeah. The ghost is accounted for." Cole said.

"Necromancer?" she asked.

"Yeah. I can talk to ghosts and raise the dead. That's why I'm here."

"Awesome. Ryan, why didn't you bring him earlier? He's really useful!"

"Ryan didn't want him involved." I answered.

"Oh. Well, okay, everyone is here do you want to start our training now or tomorrow?"

"Might as well start it now. Ryan . . ."

Ryan walked to the middle of the room and the rest of the supernaturals stood against the walls.

"Has anyone fought in a supernatural fight before?" he asked.

Five people raised their hands.

"Please step forward."

They walked out into the center with Ryan.

"What are your names, age, and supernatural species?"

"My name is Jenny. I'm a twenty-year-old vampire." the first person in the line said.

"Vlad. Twenty-five. Vampire." a black-haired man said.

"You already met me. I'm a ten-year-old warlock." James, the little boy who had opened the door earlier.

"Lynette. Twelve. Werewolf. That's my twin Sandy. She's a werewolf too." Lynette spoke for herself and her sister.

"Do all five of you think you could help me train everyone?" Ryan asked them.

They all nodded.

"Okay," he addressed the whole room again. "Jenny, Vlad, James, Lynette, and Sandy will be training you with me. Even if you are older than them, you still have to listen. Unless you want to die in combat. Your choice, of course."

Everyone mumbled. All basically agreeing that they didn't want to die.

"Grace. Where are we supposed to practice?" Ryan turned to her.

"Backyard."

"Are you kidding?"

"Have you seen my backyard?"

"No."

"Well, it was magically enlarged. Inside the fence it looks endless. And outside . . ."

"It looks puny."

"Exactly."

Ryan shrugged.

"Okay. Everybody to the backyard." he said.

When Cole and I tried to pass him he stopped us. He let everyone leave before he spoke.

"Cole do you have the armor?" he asked, eyebrows raised.

"Yes, I do." Cole answered.

"Put it on. Now."

"Wait. Where is it?" I asked.

"I already have it on. It's just a breast plate." Cole told me.

"Go put it on over your shirt." Ryan said.

I told Cole where the bathroom was and he ran off to fix his armor.

"How's he supposed to practice with a sword if it would kill everyone?" I asked Ryan.

"He'll practice on a dummy. Although, he doesn't need it."

"What do you mean?"

"He's really good with a sword. You'll see."

Cole walked into the living room wearing what looked to me like a bronze vest. I guessed that's what a breast plate was. He had a belt on now and strapped to it was a sword in a sheath on his right side, and a knife in a pouch on the other side. I assumed he was right handed and that's why his sword was on that side. His preferred weapon. Ryan nodded to me. I was right.

We walked out of the house into the backyard. It was full of supernaturals, yet there was still so much room left. They hadn't started yet, all waiting for Ryan. I saw a dummy at the side of the yard standing against the fence, a sword stuck in the ground beside it. I wondered why.

Ryan walked over to the fighters and split them into six groups. Duke and I were in his group, obviously.

Ryan's group headed to the corner of the yard closest to the house. As we were walking I noticed that Char was in our group. Paul and John were in our group too.

Ryan started by demonstrating on Duke. He showed us how to maneuver out of a hold, where to grab someone to put them to sleep, and how to anticipate the attacker's next move.

Then he paired us up to practice on each other. Duke got paired up with John. I got paired up with Paul. Char didn't have anyone so Ryan had to pair up with him.

I glanced over to see how Cole was doing. When I did I saw him sword fighting with the dummy. And the dummy was fighting back. One of the warlocks must have enchanted it for him. As I was watching he disarmed the dummy and sliced its head off.

I turned back to Paul.

"Okay. You can start." Ryan said.

Paul came at me. I quickly stepped to the right. He zoomed straight by me. I spun on my heel. His back was still to me so I darted over and flipped him. He landed face down on the ground. He jumped up and lunged. I jumped straight up and stood on his back. I jumped off and spun. He was slower than me and I quickly caught on to his fighting pattern. I was barely aware that Ryan, Char, Duke, and John had stopped and were watching Paul and me. Paul turned and dived at my feet. I danced away from his hands. He stood and I ran up and flipped him again. He landed on his back. I was standing there right when he got up. I spun him around. Knocked his knees out so he was standing on his knees. I stood on my knees, one leg across his to keep them down.

I grabbed his arms and pulled them behind his back. I held them in one hand. I grabbed his hair with the other and pulled his head back. Teeth positioned at his throat.

I got up and he fell on his face. John laughed.

"How'd I do Ryan?" I asked.

He was staring at me with his mouth gaping.

"Are you sure you've never fought before?" he asked.

"I fought Alexander when he was trying to change me. It took him an hour to get me pinned."

"You've fought him before?"

"Yeah."

"And you almost won. And this was while you were still human?"

"Yes. Ry, what is it?"

"You were born to be in battle. Born to be a vampire too."

"What?"

He motioned me to him. I helped Paul to his feet then went to Ryan. He looked me over.

"Not a scratch or bruise. Paul, how are you?" Ryan said.

"Scratched all over, my back hurts, and I have bruises from her flipping me." he held up his wrist, which was almost completely bruised; you could see distinct finger marks.

"You won't be fighting her anymore. I will."

"Thanks."

"Ashlee, come with me. The rest of you go join James's group until we get back."

They left. Ryan led me over to where Cole was practicing. Was. He had stopped to watch me fight. I looked around. *Everyone* had stopped. Out of the corner of my eye I saw Ryan nod at Cole.

I had my back to Cole. I could sense I was going to get attacked. The hairs on arms stood like I had goose bumps. I spun and caught the oncoming sword in my hand. I kicked Cole in the chest and jerked the sword out of his hand. He landed on his back. I flipped the sword so the hilt was in my hand instead of the blade. I ran up and held the tip of the sword to Cole's throat before he could get up.

I realized everyone was still staring at me. I dropped the sword to my side and helped Cole up. After he was up I handed him his sword. He looked at Ryan.

"Dude. She's got to be." Cole said.

"She's not. But she's probably related." Ryan answered, staring at me.

"Related to who?" I asked.

"Do you know anybody by the name of Phillip Prodigy?" Ryan asked.

"My grandfather's last name is Prodigy. That's on my mom's side. Why?"

"What's his first name?"

"His name is Phillip." Duke called across the yard.

"Thanks Duke." Ryan yelled back.

"What does that have to do with anything?" I asked.

"Phillip Prodigy is the only human to ever win a fight against a supernatural. It's said that he was protecting his two-year-old granddaughter. I'm assuming that's you."

I thought back to one night when I stayed with my grandpa. I was two-years-old and it was the first time that I was staying somewhere without my parents. But I had my grandpa, which was close enough. We went for a walk that night (I was a very advanced toddler; started walking and talking when I was only one and a half). It was summer and the night was oddly cold. Grandpa said he kept hearing something behind us. I thought he was joking to scare me. Then I heard it too. We both turned around and there was a blonde woman sprinting up the side walk. She had fangs. She only had eyes for me. My grandpa stood in front of me and she shrieked. He fought her and made sure he was always between me and the weird lady. Then I heard a snapping sound and the blonde lady fell to the ground, neck bend at an odd angle.

My grandpa rushed me back to his house. I never shed one tear or screamed. Just stood there and watched calmly. If someone would have seen me, they would've thought I was bored.

My grandpa told me that I was the one chosen to inherit the fighting gene. He told me stories of all the supernaturals he had fought. And that's all I thought they were: stories.

"Whoa." Ryan said.

He had been reading the memory out of my mind.

"What?" I asked.

"The gene is supposed to have dead ended with Phillip Prodigy. A girl isn't supposed to inherit, which is why your mom didn't. And I *know* Duke and Grace didn't either. No offense.

"Not *much* taken." Duke said. Grace nodded.

Ryan knelt at my feet. I was about to laugh at him, but then I saw everyone else dropping to their knees. Including my siblings.

"Why is everybody kneeling?" I asked.

"You are destined to save the world." Ryan said.

"What!?"

"It's prophesized that first girl to inherit will save the world from a terrible fate. Don't ask what the fate is because no one knows."

"Is this a joke?"

"Not at all."

I looked around. Everyone was still kneeling.

"Okay. How do I stop the kneeling thing?" I asked.

"Just order everyone to rise." Ryan said in a serious tone so I knew it wasn't a joke.

"Um. Everyone, rise!" I ordered.

Everyone stood at once. They all kept staring at me though.

"Everyone, back to training!" Ryan yelled.

Everybody went back to their groups and practiced, but they kept glancing up at me.

"We are going to win." Cole said.

"No." Ryan replied.

"If she fights Alexander . . ."

"She won't."

I looked at him.

"I *will* fight Alex." I said.

Ryan looked over. "No. You won't die, of course. But you might get hurt."

"Don't worry. I've got some things to settle with Alex. He's got a lot to pay for. I can handle him."

"Fine. Let's talk to grandfather first."

"Why?"

"He can help you train better than I can."

"Alright then. Road trip!"

Ryan turned and looked across the yard.

"Hey, Grace!" he yelled.

"What?" that was the only response he got.

"Can we borrow your car? I'll pay for the gas I use."

"Borrow the car. Don't worry about the gas."

That was easier than I thought it would be. That Mustang was Grace's baby. I guess that shows how much she trusts Ryan.

"Hey, Grace?" I yelled, "Can I drive?"

"Heck no!" she yelled back.

Ryan laughed and grabbed my hand. We ran through the house and out the front door. Right out front was Grace's Mustang. Ryan had grabbed the keys off the wall before we walked out the door. We got in the car and went on our way to grandpa's house.

CHAPTER 14
The Passing

We pulled into my grandpa's driveway. He probably heard the car but he didn't come out of the house. Grandma died a few years before I was born, so I didn't know her. My grandpa did very well on his own and didn't seem old to me.

Looking at the house, I could see that he'd kept up the flower garden we had started together. He had also painted the house some shade of off white. His old VW was in the drive in front of us. It was still dark so all I could see was the outline.

I looked down at the digital clock. It was four-o-five a.m. My grandpa was probably awake though. He liked to wake up early.

Just then, I saw, in the front room window, the curtain twitched. My grandpa was awake and knew we were here.

Ryan and I got out of the car. I met him at the walk. From there we walked up to the house together. The door swung open before we could knock. Standing in the door frame was my grandfather.

He looked a little older than the last time I'd seen him but not by much. He had the same toothy smile. Same brown hair with streaks of gray and thinning. What had changed was that he'd gotten a few inches shorter. He had also lost a few pounds which scared me. But otherwise, he was the grandpa I'd known my whole life.

"Ash Ash! You *were* coming to see me!" he said happily.

"Of course, grandpa. How'd you know?" I laughed.

I walked up and hugged him. He hugged me back. He seemed somehow fragile yet strong.

"I had a feeling that you would most likely come to me for training, seeing as you're the gene recipient. And since you are going to be going to war." my grandpa explained.

"Well, at least I don't have to explain everything." I sighed in relief.

He let go of me and ushered us through the door. We walked into the front room and sat on the couch as my grandpa ran around the house turning lights on.

As he walked into the room Ryan stood. My grandpa walked over to his old recliner, sat, then nodded at Ryan. Ryan sat back down.

"So, grandpa, you're going to train me?" I asked.

"Of course. It would be my pleasure." he nodded.

I smiled at him. I knew training with him would be a challenge. He was stubborn and had to have everything his way. Just like me. This was going to be interesting.

"Well, where are we going to train you? That's the only problem I see." grandpa said, rubbing his chin.

"We, I mean, the other fighters, are training in Grace's backyard." Ryan said.

"Grace is in town? Hmm. No one tells me anything. Very well."

He stood up and walked out of the room. Ryan and I glanced at each other then back at the doorway. My grandpa reappeared.

"Well, you kids coming?" he asked.

We stood and followed him out the door. He told us he would follow us to Grace's in his VW. I didn't argue. He had to have a way home, right?

Ryan and I were silent on the way to Grace's house. The only sound was that of the old VW following us.

When we got to Grace's Ryan pulled into the driveway and grandpa parked at the front curb. He met Ryan and me at the front door. We walked through the empty house and out the back door into the yard. Everyone stopped what they were doing to bow. Then they went back to training when grandpa nodded.

Ryan led my grandfather and me over to where Cole was taking a break. Cole stood as we approached. Grandpa nodded and he relaxed.

"Ryan, I think I need James to fix the dummy." Cole said.

He pointed at the remains of the enchanted, sword-fighting dummy. There wasn't much to see.

"James!" Ryan yelled.

James came running over. He bowed to my grandfather and me then turned to Ryan.

"What do you need?" he asked.

Ryan pointed at the dummy. "Think you can fix it?"

"With my eyes closed and without lifting my finger."

To prove his point, he did exactly that. The dummy pulled itself together and stood. He walked over and leaned against the fence.

"He needs a break though. Cole's worn him out. He'll be good in about five minutes." James told Ryan.

"Okay. Thanks. You can go back and help your group now." Ryan said.

James bowed again then took off.

"So what's going on?" Cole said, glancing at my grandpa.

"Mr. Prodigy will be training Ashlee. You could be his helper if he needs one." Ryan said.

They both looked at my grandpa.

"Of course. I would love the necromancer's help. And please, call me Phillip or Phil."

"Yes sir." Ryan and Cole said together.

I looked at them and they almost bowed to me. I guess they thought better of it and looked away.

"I'm going to go back to my group and teach." Ryan told me.

"Okay. I'll be here."

My grandpa started off different than I thought he would. Apparently, while I was talking to Ryan, he told Cole to attack me with his sword.

I felt the sword coming. By instinct I ducked then grabbed the sword out of the air. I shoved the hilt into Cole's chest and he fell backwards. I spun the sword to hold it at the hilt then positioned its point above Cole's throat.

My grandpa started laughing. I helped Cole up and handed him his sword.

"What's so funny, grandpa?" I asked.

"You're better than I thought you'd be." suddenly he got serious, "Have you ever fought a supernatural before?"

"Just the vampire that changed me."

"Did you fight him when you were still human?"

"Yes."

"Yet he still changed you?"

"We fought for an hour and I almost won. But toward the end he overpowered me."

"How old were you?"

"I was five."

"That explains why he overpowered you."

"What do you mean?"

"You were young. But you're much stronger now. I should have started your training earlier."

"Well, you can start now."

"No. You don't need it. I can't teach you something you already know. I'll go visit Duke and Grace then go home. You don't need me."

He hugged me then went off to find Duke and Grace. Cole walked up to me.

"You know what he means, right?" he asked me.

"That I can't be taught because I'm already as good as I'll get?"

"No. You've gotten better than him. When the person who inherits the gene gets better than the one who passed it. Well, let's just say, I don't think your grandpa will be able to help anymore."

"You mean, since I've 'supposedly' become a better fighter than him, he's going to . . . to die?"

"I'm sorry."

Ryan came running up to me. His eyes were watery like he was about to cry.

"I just read your grandpa's mind. You've become a better fighter than him." he said.

"I know. Cole just translated for me. Thanks." I told him.

I felt tears start to slide down my face. Ryan walked over and put his arms around me. I cried into his chest.

I heard my grandpa announce that I had surpassed him. That he was going home. That everyone was to treat me as they had treated him. He walked over to Ryan and me. I let go of Ryan to hug my grandpa. He patted my head and walked away.

I heard the car start and then listened as the sound of the engine as it traveled away from the house. I went back to crying into Ryan's chest.

*   *   *

Everyone had gone to bed after my grandpa left. The people who lived in town took off to be sure that their families wouldn't notice. I slept in Mikayla's room. Although, I didn't do much sleeping.

The phone call came at ten in the morning. Grace called me down to the kitchen. Ryan, Cole, and Duke were already there. Mikayla had offered to come with me and I let her. When I got to the kitchen and saw Grace *and* Duke crying, I felt the tears come out of my own eyes. Mikayla let me cry on her shoulder as she tried to comfort me.

"Mom said that the funeral will be next week. Friday." Grace whispered.

She sounded really hoarse. She'd been crying for a while. I nodded to her.

"Alex and Jafar are still outside your house so I'm taking you to get a dress. And Duke a suit. Ryan and Cole can get one too if they want. And Mikayla." she told me.

"Let's go now so we don't have to worry about it later." I said.

Grace grabbed her keys and we all crammed into her Mustang. Duke sat up front because he didn't like tight spaces. Cole was shoved into the driver side corner of the backseat. Ryan sat beside him, I sat beside Ryan, and Mikayla squeezed herself between me and the side of the car. Grace apologized and drove us to the mall quickly.

When we finally got the car parked, Mikayla jumped out and started running for the door. Grace had to yell at her to come back. We had to pry ourselves out of the backseat. Mikayla kept whining that we were taking too long until I glared at her. She shut up.

When we were all out Grace held on to Mikayla's shoulder like she was a little kid. We all walked into the mall together. Ryan, Cole, and Duke went to look at suits. I handed Duke two hundred dollars to buy all three suits. Grace, Mikayla, and I went to get dresses.

All three of us bought the same dress. It was a plain, straight, black dress with straps. It came with a wrap and shoes. I asked Grace if I could buy a lace long-sleeved shirt to put under it and some lace tights. She said yes and helped me find them.

After we got our clothes I called Ryan on his cell phone. He told us that he, Cole, and Duke were already out at the car. We hurried and bought the dresses. Then Grace grabbed my and Mikayla's shoulders and left the mall quickly.

We got to the car and put everyone's bags in the trunk. Then we all squeezed into the car again.

No one talked in the car. When we got back to Grace's house we got out in silence. We grabbed our bags and ran to the house. Inside, we put our outfits in the closet by the door.

"Why were you rushing so much?" I asked Grace as we sat down in the kitchen.

"I don't want Alexander and Jafar to follow you back here." she whispered.

"I thought they were still watching our house?"

"They are. I just didn't want to take any chances."

The phone rang. Grace reached over and picked it up.

"Hello? . . . Hi dad . . . . He *did*? . . . Wow . . . Okay. Thanks. Bye."

She hung up the phone.

"It has been set." she said.

"The fight?" I asked.

"Yeah. It will be next week. Saturday. The day after grandpa's funeral."

"Wonderful timing."

"That's why he chose it."

I stared out the kitchen window. I had to be the one out of a billion to carry the Prophecy. I had to be the one chosen to save the world from and unknown, terrible fate.

I sighed. "Why do I have to be the one of the Prophecy?"

"Because you were the first girl to inherit. You should be honored." Mikayla chirped.

Everyone looked at her.

"What?" she said defensively, "She asked so I answered her."

We all shrugged. Stefan walked into the room. He looked around.

"I'm sorry. Did I interrupt something?" he said blushing.

"It's okay Stefan. Come on in." I said.

"I was just here to grab a bite to eat."

"You can stay if you want."

He nodded, grabbed something out of the refrigerator, and then walked over to join Mikayla.

I hopped off the counter and walked out the backdoor. I knew Ryan would follow whether I wanted him to or not. I walked across the yard to the only tree there. I climbed up to where I was concealed from people on the ground. There I hugged my knees to my chest.

Ryan climbed up a few minutes later and sat on the branch beside mine.

"You okay?" he asked.

"I'm fine." I sighed.

"I'm sorry you have to be the heiress. And the child of Prophecy."

"It's okay, I guess. I'll just have to deal with it."

"You sound like all the natural born fighters before you."

"Well, they are my family. I should sound like them."

I looked in the yard beside my sister's. There was a family. The mother was teaching the daughter how to keep a garden. The dad was passing a football with the son.

I smiled then the backyard disappeared.

I was walking through the streets in some city I didn't recognize. The air was chilled. The streets were empty. I looked down the street both ways then continued on my way.

When I walked pass a window my reflection was mirrored. I was Alexander.

I kept walking up the street until I got to what looked like an abandoned warehouse. When I walked in the door I saw three humans walking around sorting boxes. I felt a smile on my face.

"Hey, Bill," one of the men yelled, "Where do the boxes of distributor caps go?"

"The back wall." the man named Bill answered from somewhere out of sight.

I glided up to the man who hadn't spoken. He had his back to me so it was easy to just run by him and bite him quickly in the process. I kept going as he screamed in pain. The other two came running and I bit them as they passed me. They screamed and fell to their knees. The other man had already changed and passed out.

These three men were the beginning of my new army. The other one having been destroyed by those brats. This one wouldn't be as easy for them to beat.

I opened my eyes. I was in Grace's backyard. I had just seen into the future. What I saw didn't make me feel too good. And my head hurt on top of all that. I sat up.

Ryan had me on his lap. Mikayla, Stefan, Cole, and my brother and sister were all standing around me.

"They saw you fall out of the tree and came to see if you were okay," Ryan told me, "I tried to catch you but I wasn't fast enough."

"Did I hit my head on something?" I asked rubbing it.

"Yeah. A couple braches and then a rock at the base of the tree. You feeling okay?"

"Totally. I just fell out of a tree."

"Ryan wouldn't let us take you inside. He said you couldn't be moved." Mikayla complained.

"Well, Ryan was right. If you would have moved me I would have come out of the trance."

"What trance?" Grace asked.

"I can see into the future. Usually I have to make myself see it. This time it happened by itself."

"What did you see?" Ryan asked.

"Alexander. Well, I saw it as if I *was* Alexander. He was building *another* army. We destroyed his first and I'm guessing he got away."

I thought of the vision and Ryan watched. His face paled as he watched Alex change the three humans.

"Well, isn't it good that we beat his first army?" Mikayla asked.

"Not when he gets away and builds an even stronger army." Ryan sighed.

He looked defeated.

"We *will* kill him in the end." I told him.

He smiled. He trusted my judgment and knew I wasn't just saying that to make him feel better. I meant it.

"We should get everyone here and continue training." he told Grace.

"I'll go call the people who aren't staying at the house." she told him, "Mikayla, go get the others out of their rooms."

Mikayla gave her a salute and ran into the house. Grace followed at a slower pace. I turned to Ryan.

"What am I supposed to do while you guys train?" I asked.

"Practice on the other dummy." Ryan said pointing at the two dummies against the fence.

"Okay."

"By the way, I've thought of some strategies. Want to hear them?"

"Sure."

"You know Cole can raise the dead, right?"

"Right."

"Well, when we see the size of the enemy army we can get more fighters if we need them."

"How?"

"Cole will raise the dead and they will fight for our side. However many Alex can gather, we will still have more than him."

"Okay. Wouldn't raising the dead take a lot of concentration?"

"That's where you come in. Cole will give you his sword and you will protect him while he raises them. You know how to wield a sword, right?"

"Kind of. It's more instinctional than knowing."

"Well, use your natural instinct to protect him until he is done. Then you have to go after Alexander."

"Got it."

Training that day was different for me. I practiced with Cole. He gave me his sword to practice with first. Said I was a natural then handed me his knife. He said only the best can fight with a knife because knives limit you more because they are shorter. After practicing with the knife for at least ten minutes he said I was too good at that too. There was no reason for me to practice.

I walked over to one of the lawn chairs and watched the rest of the fighters train. I guess that was how it would be until the fight. Me sitting in a lawn chair, doing nothing while everyone else was training. Fun.

CHAPTER 15
The Prophecy

I t was Friday. The day of my grandfather's funeral. Tomorrow was the fight. I woke up early in the morning and got dressed in my black lace tights, black lace shirt under my plain black dress.

I went to the kitchen. Everyone else was still sleeping. I fixed enough breakfast for everyone in the house then went room to room telling everyone to go down to the kitchen for breakfast. After that was done I walked back to the kitchen and got four trays out of the cabinet.

I packed the trays full of breakfast food. I told Mikayla to help me carry them. She took two from me then followed me out of the kitchen and up the stairs.

We went to the room that Ryan, Cole, and Duke were sharing. I opened the door with my foot and walked in, followed by Mikayla. I flipped the lights on and all the boys groaned.

"Fine. If you don't want this food I guess we'll just leave. Come on Mikayla." I said.

The three boys sat up fast enough to give themselves headaches.

"Sorry. We love you girls. We do want the food." Ryan said holding his head.

The other two nodded. Mikayla took one tray to Cole and the other to Duke. I took one of mine to Ryan.

"Who's the other one for?" he asked.

"Grace. I'll go give it to her now. I'll be back." I said and started to leave.

"Hey, Ashlee." Ryan said softly, "Thanks for the food. And you look great, even though you are wearing black."

I smiled at him then left the room. I went to Grace's room and knocked on the door then opened it. She was sitting up rubbing her eyes. I told her to close them and turned the lights on. I carried the tray to her. She opened her eyes and smiled at me. I laid the tray across her lap. Then I sat at the end of her bed.

"Thanks Ashlee." she said through a mouthful of food.

I laughed at her.

"I'll be back up with your dress." I told her.

She nodded.

I got up and went to the closet by the door. Mikayla had taken her dress and was probably wearing it around the house. I grabbed the three suits and Grace's dress.

I took Grace her dress before I took the suits up.

"Thanks," she told me. "Just lay it over that chair."

I did as she said.

"I can't believe that the fight is tomorrow. I can't believe grandpa's gone." she mumbled.

I went over to her and hugged her. She told me she would meet me in the living room. I left her room and went to the guys' room. They had finished their food already. That didn't surprise me.

I handed out the suits. I didn't have to ask whose was whose. I just went by sizes. Duke put his on as soon as handed it to him. So did Ryan. Cole left to go change in the bathroom.

"He's shy. He won't change in front of Duke either. Only me." Ryan told me.

"Makes sense. You are his twin brother." I said.

"Yeah. He hasn't known you two long enough to be himself yet. Just give him some time."

I nodded.

I walked up to Duke to fix his hair and jacket. Ryan crossed the room behind me to look in the mirror. He was trying to tie his tie. Duke handed me his and I tied it for him and straightened it. Then I walked over to where Ryan had his tied in knots. I untied the knots then tied it right and straightened it. Ryan blushing the whole time.

Cole walked back into the room. Tie hanging around his neck, untied. He walked over to his bed and sat down.

"Does anybody know how to tie these stupid things?" he asked.

Duke and Ryan pointed to me. I walked over to Cole and tied it. He was, at least, able to straighten it himself.

"Okay. We have to meet Grace and Mikayla in the living room." I said.

I put my arm around Duke's shoulders and led him out of the room. Ryan and Cole followed. Grace and Mikayla were waiting for us. When we walked in they stood and we walked out the front door together.

"Hey, Grace," I said. "Did dad say where the fight was going to be?"

"An abandoned farmland." she answered.

I nodded.

We all crammed into the Mustang again and headed to the funeral home. We were supposed to meet my mom and dad in the parking lot.

When we pulled in we parked beside their car. They were still in it. They got out when we did.

My mom looked between Ryan and Cole.

"They're twins, mom." I whispered to her.

She laughed and smiled at them. It was a tight laugh and a forced smile. Her dad had unexpectedly died. Of course she wouldn't laugh and smile like usual. I hugged her. Then I walked over to my dad and hugged him.

"Good luck tomorrow, kiddo." he whispered in my ear.

"Thanks dad." I whispered back.

He let go of me and we all walked into the funeral home together.

The home's décor made it look like a place for a happy gathering instead of a place for mourning. That only made it more depressing. There were flowers from mourners everywhere. The walls were painted bright yellow and the carpet was neon orange. The whole place smelled like cheap, old lady perfume. I almost gagged when I smelled it, but I knew that would upset my mother even more than the cheery colors. Why someone would deck out a funeral home like that, I had no clue. Unless they were insane.

"I'm going to go put the writhe by the casket." my mom said.

She walked away and my father followed her.

"I'm not going near the casket." I told Ryan.

"We can't anyway." he said sadly.

"What do you mean?"

"Vampires can't go near caskets if they have dead humans in them."

"Why not?"

"It's kind of like there is a barrier that we can't cross. I think it's to be respectful. Vampires and humans don't get along well. So the Royals set up boundaries."

"So, Grace and I can't even see our grandfather?"

"No. Duke can't either. It's the same for werewolves. Look at your father."

I looked he was standing twenty feet from the casket as if he couldn't move any closer.

"That's not right. He is family. We should be allowed to go near him." I said.

"Supernatural rules have no exceptions." Ryan sighed.

I walked into the viewing area and went to where my dad was standing. He put his arm around my shoulders and held me to his side. It looked like he was comforting me. He was actually keeping me from trying to get to the casket.

I understood that even if I did make it to the casket something bad would happen to me as a punishment.

My mom walked over to the casket and leaned in to kiss her father on the forehead. The only part of him that I could see was the tip of his nose.

Everyone froze. It looked like they were statues. I looked around. A man was throwing his daughter up in the air and catching her. The little girl was frozen in the air. Everyone was quiet as if time had stopped. I looked back at the casket. When I did I saw movement.

My dead grandpa sat up in his casket and turned his head to look at me.

He spoke in someone else's voice. A woman's raspy voice:

"The first female to inherit shall save the world. A terrible fate lies ahead. She must kill and grieve and suffer losses. She must always lose to gain. The road ahead of her is difficult and full of pain. She shall choose to rule or destroy."

My grandpa lay back down in his casket and everyone unfroze.

"Dad," I said slowly, "Did you just see that?"

"See what?" he asked, raising an eyebrow.

"Never mind. I need to go talk to Ryan."

I ducked under his arm and walked over to Ryan. He had stayed where I had left him. Grace, Cole, Duke, and Mikayla had gone in the room across the hallway to mingle and mourn with family members. As I approached Ryan frowned.

"Are you okay?" he asked.

"Did you see what just happened?"

"You walked over to your dad, he hugged you, your mom kissed her father's forehead, and then you walked back here."

"Okay. So you didn't see."

"See what?"

He looked extremely worried.

"My grandpa just sat up in his casket and talked to me in a woman's voice." I said.

Ryan's eyes widened. "What did she say?"

I repeated, word for word, what the woman's voice had said. Ryan's eyes widened even more.

"Why are you looking at me like that?" I demanded.

"Because. One of the Royals just spoke to you through your grandpa."

"Um, okay. But I understood nothing of what she said."

"She just told you the *whole* prophecy that involves you. I'll think about it and translate it to you later."

I nodded.

We walked into the room that the other four had disappeared in. When we walked in I looked around for our group. As I did I nodded at people who looked familiar. Then I spotted Grace and the others on the other side of the room. Ryan and I squeezed our way over to them. As we got closer to them they looked up. All their gazes shifted to me and they all donned worried expressions.

Ryan told them about the prophecy. He left out how I received it.

"What does it mean?" Grace asked.

"All I know is that it doesn't sound too good." Ryan told her.

We all nodded.

I was beginning to understand the prophecy now. But I would tell Ryan later.

I was the first female to inherit the gene. I would have to save the world from a terrible fate or I would suffer a terrible fate. I would have to kill people to save the world and I would feel guilty about it and I would lose some of the people I knew and loved. I would have to lose people to gain power. There would be many challenges and I would get hurt overcoming them. And I would choose to destroy the supernatural world or to rule it.

Ryan's head snapped up in my direction. He had been reading my mind.

"You're right." he whispered in a strained voice.

The others looked at him weird.

"She just figured out what the prophecy means." he explained.

They all looked at me.

"I decide the fate of myself, my friends, my enemies, and the supernatural world itself." I whispered.

All of their eyes widened. I realized the prophecy had already started.

"It's started?" Ryan repeated.

"I'm the heiress. I have to save the world from Alexander. I'm going to end up killing a lot of his army. I will lose some friends in the fight, and I've already lost my grandpa. I will lose whoever I lose as I gain power. The challenges will be set up by Alex and, of course, they will hurt me. Plus, I'm sure the Royals are going to have their part in it. And when it's over I'll have enough power to destroy the supernatural world, but I have to choose to rule or destroy it."

They all stared at me.

"What?" I asked.

"How did you figure out the prophecy so quickly?" Ryan asked.

"It wasn't that hard. But the way I see it, you five are part of the prophecy too."

They all exchanged glances. Then all five of them kneeled at my feet.

"We are yours to order. We are a permanent part of your army." Ryan said, speaking for the five of them.

I nodded.

"Rise." I ordered.

They all stood up.

I was already gaining power. I would start losing tomorrow.

*   *   *

We joined the cars behind the hearse. We followed through the middle of town and through the cemetery. We pulled over when my parents did. We all got out of the car and followed the hearse by foot the rest of the way.

Family surrounded the grave for the burial ceremony. I had to lean on Ryan because I felt worn out. I grabbed his wrist and looked at his watch. It was only four in the afternoon. I dropped his hand and yawned discreetly.

After the burial was done we lay flowers on the fresh grave as we left. We crammed into Grace's car and went to her house.

CHAPTER 16
Final Preparations

I woke up at seven Saturday morning. My sister was already up so I helped her fix breakfast for the whole house plus the people who were coming over.

After we had breakfast fixed I went upstairs to get Cole's sword. The boys didn't even flinch. I told Grace I was going to practice in the backyard. She said she'd tell Cole I had his sword so he wouldn't freak out.

I fought with the dummy for two hours straight and didn't even break a sweat. But I couldn't say much for the dummy.

As I was getting ready to fight the other dummy, I heard a voice behind me.

"I see you stole my sword."

Cole.

I swung the sword and sliced the dummy's sword hand off. The sword clattered to the ground. I let the dummy pick it up then I parried his strike and sliced his chest open. He tried to slice my throat but I ducked. Then, with a swipe of the sword, I cut the second dummy's head off.

I turned to see Cole sitting in the lawn chair.

"Sorry. You were asleep and I wanted to practice." I told him.

"It's okay. You haven't been able to practice much. We've been telling you that you don't need it."

"So you understand that I *want* to train?"

"Yeah. But I still don't think you need it."

I looked down at the dummies.

"Is James awake?" I asked.

"Yes. But I don't think you should practice anymore."

"Why not?"

"Have you eaten breakfast?"

"Well, no. Why?"

He laughed. "You need to eat. Your sister fixed an extra bloody steak just for you."

My stomach growled. Cole laughed. He had heard it.

"Come on. Go inside and eat." he said.

I walked away from the dummies and followed Cole into the kitchen. Everyone stood when I walked in the door. I nodded and they sat back down.

My sister took the sword out of my hand and gave me a plate. The steak was oozing blood and I swear I heard it say '*moo.*'

I sucked the blood out of the steak and I was full. Blood was more filling than human food. I also felt even stronger. I also realized I needed to try fighting both the dummies at once.

When I told Cole he agreed. We found James and he fixed the dummies. Cole had given me a shield to use too. He sat in the lawn chair and waited for my practice to begin.

James told me that he'd enchanted the dummies to go after me way more than they had been. They'd been enchanted for Cole and apparently that was too 'easy' for me. James left the backyard and went into the kitchen.

"Good luck." Cole told me.

I nodded and the dummies attacked at the same time.

One dummy went to my right, the other to my left. I kicked the one on my right in the chest and disarmed the one on my left. As the one I'd kicked was still down, I sliced off the disarmed dummy's head. His body fell to the ground. By that time the other dummy had gotten up. I parried his strike, sliced his chest, and disarmed him. As he lunged for his sword, I sliced his head off.

I turned to Cole. He was sitting forward in the chair, eyes wide, and his mouth hanging open.

"You *definitely* don't need practice." he said.

"Oh, come on. You're looking at me as if I just slapped you."

"You should have seen yourself. You would have the same look on your face."

I handed him his sword, hilt forward. Then I left him staring after me as I walked back in the house.

Everyone stood again. I nodded. They sat. I found Ryan in the living room and walked up to him.

"You might want to go get your brother and bring him inside." I said.

"Why?" Ryan stood up fast, "Did something happen to him?"

"No. He's sitting in that lawn chair obsessing over the way I took on the two dummies at once."

"You took both of them at once?"

"Yes."

James walked in the room.

"I also amped them up to be more of a challenge. Apparently, I didn't amp them up enough." he told Ryan.

"Don't worry about it. I'm done practicing." I said.

"I'll go repair them so that Cole can practice."

He turned and left the room.

"When's the fight supposed to start?" I asked.

"Around two in the afternoon." Ryan answered.

"What time is it now?"

He looked at his watch. "Eleven thirty-one."

I nodded. I didn't like that we were so close to a fight that would take many lives. But then again I couldn't do anything about it. And I definitely couldn't stop it.

* * *

At noon, we headed to the farmland that was the battle ground. We positioned our stronger fighters to surround the weaker ones. We took the shape of a rectangle and faced every direction. Not knowing which way they'd come from was a disadvantage.

I was positioned beside Cole. When the enemy came into sight I would take his sword and keep them off of him. He would raise the dead to fight for us.

After he did that, I would go after Alexander. He would be positioned behind his army, out of harm's way. I would take Jafar down too. I would have to to get to Alexander. I knew she would be wherever he was.

I turned to Cole.

"You ready?" he asked.

"Not really. But I do wish they would get here soon." I said.

"Well, it's actually our fault. We are two hours early."

"Just to be prepared."

"Oh, I know. They definitely won't be expecting this."

"Yeah. Let's just hope they get so distracted that our best fighters can kill them before they realize what's going on."

He nodded.

I looked around for Ryan. He was still positioning people. Then I found the position he had chosen to leave empty for himself. The middle of the front line. He was one of our best fighters, except for me. But I was to stay in the middle to protect Cole. At least until Cole could protect himself again.

I picked up Cole's wrist and looked at his watch, then dropped it. It was one-forty. Only twenty minutes until the fight.

I could feel them coming. My natural fighting instincts told me which way they would come from.

"Ryan! You set us up wrong!" I called.

He looked over at me. "Which way are they going to come from?"

"The other side of this field. They'll come in on our right and back if we stay where we are."

Ryan quickly repositioned everyone. When he was done he asked me if we'd be good now. I nodded, but I wasn't so sure. The position was good. But were our fighters?

"Time?" I asked Cole.

"One-fifty-five."

I nodded.

Five more minutes and the fight would be upon us.

I glared into the trees. I felt them getting closer. It felt, kind of, like you would imagine tight spaces for someone who is claustrophobic. The closer the enemy got, the more it felt like my lungs were being compressed.

"They're almost here. Ready yourselves." I shouted.

At my command, everyone stood erect. All tensed, waiting for the attack.

Then the enemy broke through the tree line. At least fifty.

CHAPTER 17

Blood, War, and Lies

I looked at Cole. He nodded and handed me his sword. I looked around as the fight broke out. The enemy had moved past our first line. I saw Ryan fighting a red-headed girl, as I watched he snapped her neck.

I felt someone approaching Cole. I spun around fast. Cole was standing there with his eyes closed and hands up, palms facing in front of him.

The person, who was running at Cole, was a little girl. A little vampire girl. She didn't stop to think, just kept running at him.

Cole's shield, which had been at his feet, floated up. The girl ran into it and knocked herself out.

The ghost was helping me.

Someone approached behind me now. I turned and slashed at the oncoming vampire. I ended up miscalculating and sliced his arm off. That made him mad. He came at me, fangs bared. I sliced with the sword. This time his head fell to the ground.

Two more vampires came up behind me. I turned, holding out the sword. One got his head chopped off; the other got her shoulder sliced open. She ran at me and I swung the sword. Her head fell by the others.

I backed up so I was two inches from Cole. I saw the shield slam into a boy's face. When the boy landed on the ground the ghost snapped his neck.

I looked around the battle field. There were dead supernatural creatures everywhere.

The ground shook and everyone stopped fighting long enough to see the earth split open under their feet. Everyone went back to their fights as the bodies of one hundred dead people crawled out of the chasm.

Someone tapped my shoulder. I looked before I swung the sword. Cole was done.

I handed him the sword and the ghost brought him his shield. He thanked us both then ran off to lead his army of the dead. I looked around to see if anyone needed help. My eyes went directly to Ryan.

He was on the ground. Jafar was standing over him. He didn't look like he could get up. Jafar raised her hand and I saw a silver dagger.

I ran at her. We both fell to the ground. I rolled so she was pinned to the ground underneath me. I wrestled with her to get the dagger, slit her throat, and got up.

I ran to Ryan but he motioned me away as he got up. He mumbled a thanks then took off.

I looked at the ground where Jafar had been. She was gone. I hadn't killed her. I just made her *really* mad.

I ran through the fights, occasionally helping people if they needed it. When I passed a couple wolves I realized that they had forced themselves to Change.

I found Cole. He was pressed to the ground. Defending himself with his shield and swinging his sword like a lunatic. I ran over and jumped on his vampire attacker's back. I bit into his throat. He let out a piercing scream right before I snapped his neck.

I helped Cole up. He thanked me and I went running around the battle ground again.

Someone started running at me from behind. I spun to face them. I stood tensed, ready for him to attack me. Ready to kill him. At the last second the vampire got confused and stopped.

As I was about to jump him, he spoke.

"Ashlee? Is that you?" he asked, head tilted to the side.

I froze.

"Who are you and how do you know me?" I growled.

"So you are Ashlee?"

"So?"

"I'm Jimmy. You're my twin sister."

"I only have two siblings. And they are on my side of this."

"You don't know me because your dad kept me a secret."

"Well, wouldn't my mother notice?"

"No. Our mother is dead."

"Um, no. I live with *my* mother."

"Yes. That one *is* alive. I'm talking about our birth mother."

"I'm just supposed to believe you?"

The battle was getting more and more intense. I could hear blood curdling screams everywhere. Everywhere I looked I saw blood. There were distinctive colors of blood. Here and there was werewolf blood, red like a human's. There was also blood of the magical beings: black blood. Then there was the silver blood; the blood of a vampire.

"You shouldn't believe me," Jimmy said, "But if you just read my mind, you will know that I'm not lying."

I thought about it for a second.

"Would you seriously let me read your mind? Willingly?" I asked.

"Yes. I will also protect you while you do."

I stared into his eyes and read his mind whether I wanted to or not. The noises of battle faded until they were nonexistent.

I was alone in a house that looked like it hadn't been inhabited for years. I looked around. I was waiting for someone.

The door opened and a man walked in carrying five large bags. I got up and ran over to help him. It was my dad. He gave me a one-armed hug.

We carried the bags to the kitchen. A thick coat of dust covered everything. I sat the bags on the counter.

"Did you bring me anything?" I said.

My voice was Jimmy's. I was Jimmy.

"Of course." my father said.

He got in his wallet and took out a picture. He handed it to me and I examined it. It was me.

"She's pretty. She looks almost exactly like me." I told my father.

"You are twins. You should look alike."

"Thanks for the picture dad. But I would like to meet her in person. Could you arrange that?"

"No son."

"Why not?"

"Because you are in hiding. My wife doesn't even know you exist. She doesn't even know that Ashlee isn't really hers."

"I would still like to meet her in person."

"Maybe someday. But for now you have to stay a secret."

My father kissed the top of my head then patted me on the back. He walked out the door and left me alone.

I looked up at Jimmy. He hadn't let anyone kill me, which was a good sign.

"You really are my twin brother." I said.

"Yes." he answered.

"Well, what about my mom? The one that is alive. How does she not know?"

"You'll have to ask dad."

I nodded.

"I would like to join your side. But I can't fight." he whispered.

"If you join our side you have to fight."

"I could sit out. If I try to fight with you your side won't know and they'll kill me. Or Alexander's army will say I'm a traitor and kill me."

"Fine. You can join our side and sit out."

"Thanks. And you should know, the mom you have been living with is really your aunt."

He ran off leaving me with that.

I felt that someone was running toward me so I turned. A young boy was attacking me, his fangs bared.

I raised my stolen dagger as the boy got closer.

I remembered what Cole had said. Only the best can fight with a knife in the place of a sword. I hoped I was as good as everyone said.

I shoved the dagger into the boy's right eye and he screamed. I jerked the dagger out and jabbed him in the left eye. Now my opponent was blind. I stabbed him in the heart. His breath caught and he fell to the ground.

I grabbed the dagger and walked away.

As I was looking for Alexander, two more vampires attacked me. I fought them with fist and dagger. I'd injured both of them badly but they wouldn't back off. Then I felt someone coming at me from behind me. No way could

I take these two *and* the one coming. I was dead.

That's when I heard a growl.

STAY AWAY FROM MY SISTER! Duke shouted in my mind.

I looked over my shoulder and saw his jaws clamp down around my new attacker's body. He died when my brother's fangs sank into his skull.

I went back to my two injured attackers. They were distracted so I sliced the girl's head off. The man screamed. It was cut short when I sliced his head off too.

I walked away from them. If I kept getting attacked by every vampire enemy I passed I would never find Alex. And that's the very reason they were all attacking me.

I walked back in the direction I had come from. Only one vampire attacked. I easily cut off his head.

I turned around. About one hundred yards from the battle, a farmhouse stood between us and the road. It seemed like the closer I got to the house, there were more vampires attacking me. If I walked away from the house only one vampire would attack me. If I was just standing still all they did was watch me, trying to guess what I would do next.

I knew what I had to do. I had to find Ryan and Cole.

*   *   *

Ryan, Cole, and I stood in the middle of the battle field. We were discussing my idea.

"So you are sure he's down there?" Ryan asked.

"No. I told you. I *think* he's down there. Every time I get closer to the farmhouse a bunch of fighters attack me."

"She's right Ryan. I've been watching." Cole said. "She just took on three attacks right before she found us."

"Okay. So what's your idea again?" Ryan turned to me.

"I need you two to come with me." I said.

"What do we have to do?"

"Well, the closer I get to the house more attackers come. If I get close enough there will be too many for me to take on my own. If I have you two come with me you could help me when it gets to that point."

They looked at each other and nodded.

"So you're in?" I asked.

They both nodded again.

"Okay. Let's do this." I said.

We started walking toward the house. Two vampires stepped in front of us. One was Jimmy. I glared at him and he shook his head. The other guy had dragged him out here.

I stabbed the other guy in the stomach with my dagger and he doubled over.

"Jimmy, could you help us now?" I asked.

He nodded and moved behind me.

I stabbed the man, who was still bent over, in the head.

"Who is this?" Ryan asked pointing at Jimmy.

"That's my twin brother. Jimmy. He's on our side so don't kill him." I answered.

Ryan frowned at me. I'd have to explain it all to him later.

"What are you guys doing?" Jimmy asked.

"We're trying to get to that house. Alexander is in it."

"Leave it to him to hide while everyone else is fighting."

I nodded.

We ran this time. We made it five feet before being attacked again. Three vampires stood in front of us. I looked at Ryan and Cole and nodded.

They attacked the other two and left me with the little girl.

The little girl sprang at me. I stepped aside but she still landed on her feet. I was turned around before she could defend herself. I went at her with the dagger. She turned in time to see the dagger plunge into her chest. I jerked the dagger out as she fell.

I looked over. Cole and Ryan had killed their opponents. We nodded at each other then took off running again.

We got to the edge of the battle field and suddenly we had five vampires surrounding us. Our four to their five. I would have to take two. Jimmy, whether he liked it or not, had to fight.

Jimmy looked at me and nodded. He knew what I was thinking and he was telling me I didn't have to say it.

Ryan and Cole jumped onto their opponents. Jimmy lunged at his. I stared at my two.

One was a teenage boy. He reminded me of Ryan the first day I had met him. The other was an older man, he kind of reminded me of Ryan's father.

The older one lunged at my neck while the young one lunged at my feet. I danced out of the young one's reach then tried to stab the old one. The dagger went into his shoulder. I jerked it out quickly. The boy came at me while the older man held his bloody shoulder. I slammed my dagger into the boy's skull. He fell to the ground and I took the dagger. The man screamed and ran at me. I raised my dagger. When he got close enough I shoved it in his chest.

I looked at the boys. They were staring at me. I raised my eyebrows. Ryan and Cole shrugged.

We ran across the field toward the house. Once we were off the battle field no one attacked us. Everyone was behind us in the crowd of people. The enemy would have to fight their way out to attack us again.

We were five yards from the house when the others stopped. I looked at them.

"This is as far as we are going." Ryan said.

I raised an eyebrow.

"This is your fight, not ours." Cole explained, "Good luck."

He walked up and hugged me. Ryan coughed. Cole let go and walked back to the battle field to lead his army of the dead.

Jimmy walked up and patted my back. Then he followed Cole to the battle.

Ryan moved closer to me. I looked up at him.

"I wish I could go with you. Just in case . . . something happens. You know?" he whispered.

"Don't worry about me." I told him, "I'll be fine. Alexander is nothing. Just don't get yourself killed by distracting yourself with me."

I stood on my toes and kissed him on the cheek. Then I left him there. I walked toward the house. When I reached the porch I looked back.

Ryan was still there. He had tears running down his face. He waved then ran off to join the fight again. I raised my hand in a wave, but it was too late. He had already disappeared.

I turned back to the house.

It was a really worn down old house. It looked like it was from the 1930's. Paint was peeling off the outside walls. The window shutters were either hanging crooked or had already fallen off. I looked at the porch. Parts of it were falling in, the rest of it was rotted. The steps looked like they would fall in if a feather landed on them.

I walked up the steps. They didn't even creak. I looked for a good place to step onto the porch. There wasn't any good spots. So instead of taking my chances with human speed, I ran across the porch to the door at vampire speed. I had made it.

I opened the door. I thought it would creak. It didn't.

The door opened into a hallway. That hallway had two doors on the left, three doors on the right, and a set of steep, narrow stairs at its end.

I thought about checking inside the doors but my gut told me to go up the stairs. In a fight like this I decided I should listen to my gut.

I crept down the hallway. At the foot of the stairs I was able to hear voices. Two people arguing. I recognized them as Jafar and Alexander's voices. I walked carefully up the stairs.

Half way up, the stairway opened into a small landing with a door on the right. I knew the voices were further up so I didn't bother looking in the room. I started up the stairs again but something stopped me. A moaning sound came from the room on the landing.

I went back down to it and pressed my ear to the door. The moaning sound came again. I slowly opened the door and walked in. At first all I saw was an empty, old bedroom.

There was an old four-poster bed. The canopy hanging over it was tattered and had moth holes. An old school desk was sitting in one of the corners. There was one window with the glass panes knocked out. The room was covered in a thick layer of dust.

When I looked closer I saw someone under the bed. The person moaned. I could tell it was a girl.

I ran up to the side of the bed and dropped on my knees. I looked at the girl; she looked about Duke's age. She reminded me of the girl he had a crush on too. A little too much like her to be coincidence.

"Marie?" I asked.

The girl looked at me. She frowned.

"Ash-lee?" she choked out.

"Yeah. What are you doing?"

"Hiding."

"From who?"

"That man with the fangs. He bit me."

"Alexander?"

"He didn't say his name."

"Are you thirsty?"

She nodded.

"But you don't want water?" I asked.

She shook her head.

I had heard that if a new vampire was this weak and hungry you could give it some of your own blood. I'd never tried it of course. Might as well try now.

I put my wrist by her mouth. She looked up at me, her eyebrows knitting together.

"Bite. Just make sure it's on a vein." I told her.

She licked her lips nervously. She looked confused but she listened to me.

She bit into one of my smaller veins and she hit it dead on. It didn't even hurt me. I could feel the blood leave my body but it quickly regenerated. After a few seconds I figured she had had enough. I didn't know how my blood would affect her.

I tapped on her jaw. She released my wrist, blushing and looking away. I put my hand on her shoulder.

"It's okay." I told her.

"What am I?" she asked. Her voice was stronger.

"You're a vampire." I didn't stall; she deserved to know.

"Those are real?"

"Yes. I'm one."

"I thought vampires didn't have blood and that's why they drink it?"

I held up my arm to show her my wrist. Silver blood was running down my arm. You could see the open bite mark. I remembered hearing that if a vampire licked a cut it would seal itself and heal.

I raised my wrist to my mouth and licked the bite marks. They sealed instantly and I could see them healing under the blood. I reached down and wiped the blood on my jeans without looking.

"You know you're covered in that silver stuff?" Marie asked.

"It's vampire blood."

"Well, you're covered in it."

I looked down. There were splashes and smears of silver blood all over my jeans and there was some on my shirt but not as much. I looked back at her.

"It's from the battle." I explained.

"What battle?" she asked.

"Never mind. Don't worry about that now."

"Is that *your* blood?"

"No."

She nodded.

"I have something to take care of. You stay here and I'll come back for you when I'm done." I told her.

"Okay." she said in a small voice.

"Stay hidden and don't make any noise."

She nodded. I got up and walked out of the room.

On the landing I heard Jafar and Alexander arguing again. I followed their voices up the stairs. I came to a small hallway. There was one room on the left and on the right. At the end of the hallway was a metal ladder leading into an open square doorway. The ladder was rusted and the black paint was chipping off. It was obvious where it led. The attic.

Leave it to Alexander to bring the stereotype of vampires and attics into this.

I walked over to the ladder and started climbing. Before I got to the opening I stopped. I listened to see where they were in the room above. I didn't want to climb up there with my back to them.

As I had suspected, they were behind me. I turned on the ladder and climbed up. I lifted myself up into the attic and stood quickly.

I was facing Alexander and Jafar. Alex was sitting in an old fashioned sitting room chair wrapped in plastic. Jafar was sitting on the floor beside him. Both were looking at me.

Alexander had a cruel smile on his face. Jafar only glared at me. Dried silver blood was still on her throat but I could see that she had had someone heal it. She probably didn't like the fact that she had to have help.

Alexander looked me over to see if any harm had been done to me. When he found no injuries he frowned. He looked confused and mad. Confused because he didn't know how I went through his guards without getting a scratch on me. Mad because I was alive.

He looked down at Jafar. She shook her head.

Alex got up and walked over to the window that faced the battle field. He had his back to me. It seemed like a perfect opportunity. Only I could see that it wasn't. Being the receiver of the gene I could see what would happen.

If I attacked him now Jafar would jump on me. She would take the dagger I had stolen from her and shove it into my skull. Alexander wouldn't even turn around. He didn't care about her.

Alexander turned to me. He looked down at Jafar and nodded. She got up and went to the window. Alex looked back at me.

"Your fighters have defeated my army, granddaughter of Prodigy." he growled, glaring at me.

I nodded sharply.

He turned toward Jafar. Perfect opportunity. I raised the dagger and ran at him quietly and quickly. Jafar turned as I advanced. Her eyes widened and she jumped between Alexander and me. I cut her throat and stabbed her in the chest. I missed her heart but got her lung. Alexander looked down at her.

"Alex . . . Help me!" Jafar gasped.

"I'm sorry, dear. I no longer require your assistance. You mean nothing to me. Good-bye." he turned into a bat and flew out the open window.

I looked down at Jafar; she was looking at me. She was crying. I felt a little sorry for her. She had stayed behind Alexander then she gave her life to save his. And she asked for him to help her, he called her meaningless, and then runs (flies) away.

"Just . . . Kill me." she pleaded.

I frowned.

But I did want she wanted. I shoved the blade of the silver dagger into her heart. Silver blood spilled everywhere when I took the blade out. She lay motionless on the attic floor.

I climbed back down the ladder and ran down to the landing with the old bed room. I went in the room and walked over to the bed. Marie crawled out. She looked at my clothes.

"You have more blood on you." she pointed out.

"Yeah. I just killed someone." I told her, "Come on, let's get out of here.

We left the room. We ran down the stairs, down the hallway, and straight out the front door. I didn't even worry about the rotted porch. We just kept running until we got to the field.

The dead had returned into the earth. There were dead bodies all over the field. A shimmer appeared beside me. The ghost wanted me to follow it.

It took me over to a group of people. I pushed my way through them, Marie right on my heels.

When I got to the center I saw two identical boys. One was lying on the ground with his head in the other's lap. Ryan and Cole. Cole was the one on the ground. I ran up and fell to my knees beside them. He was still breathing.

"What happened?" I asked.

"He passed out. Raising the dead, controlling them, and then sending them back took a lot out of him." Ryan told me.

I nodded. When I did I saw his arm bent at an odd angle.

"Is his arm broken?" I asked pointing.

Ryan looked down and mumbled something.

"Yeah, it's broken." he answered, "Think you can set it?"

I nodded.

I set his arm. Then ripped a piece of my shirt and took off my shoe. I made a makeshift splint for his arm. Ryan thanked me.

"So . . . How'd it go with Alexander?" he asked me.

CHAPTER 18
The Return of an Old Friend

Ryan was upset about Alexander just leaving Jafar to die. He thought Alexander was a coward. He wasn't wrong. We walked around the battle field. All our dead enemies were gone. Cole had put them in the earth when he returned the dead fighters he had raised. We were looking now to see if there were injured people among the dead.

We only found four injured people shielding themselves with dead bodies. James, Paul, John, and Duke were the injured.

We took them over to Mr. Watson. He had a doctor's degree and, thank God, he had survived the battle. James, Paul, and John were easy for him to fix up. Duke, however, was harder.

Duke had gotten hurt while he was a wolf so Mr. Watson had to set the bones as you would a dog's. Seeing as he was a werewolf too, he knew how the bones went.

Cole walked up to me. He was up, which was good. The bad thing was that he was really pale and clammy. I had to catch him as he got closer because he almost collapsed at my feet. I helped him onto his feet.

"Are you okay?" I asked.

"Yeah. Still a little worn out from the extreme necromancy I had to do." he answered wiping his forehead.

"If you need to, lean on me. I don't want you to fall."

He nodded and leaned on me. I held most of his weight but I didn't mind. He wasn't light, but he wasn't heavy either, so he was easy to hold up.

Ryan walked over to me. He looked like he'd been crying again. He nodded to Cole but kept looking at me.

"We lost a lot of people." he told me.

"How many do we still have?" I asked.

"Not counting us? About twelve."

"Can you make a list?"

"Yeah. I'll get some paper out of the farmhouse."

I nodded.

Cole looked to his right. I followed his eyes and saw a shimmer standing right beside him.

"I told you I would. But I'm too weak right now. It will have to be later." he told it.

The shimmer moved in front of me. Cole's eyes followed it. It wrapped around me. I almost freaked out but supporting Cole stopped me from jerking away.

"She's just giving you a hug. It's okay." he explained to me.

"Who is she?" I asked.

He looked at the shimmer, which was in front of him now.

"She is Karla Case." he told me.

"What did she want you to do?"

"Bring her back."

"You can do that?"

"With all the deaths I caused here? Yeah, I can."

"Is it like a life for a life kind of thing?"

"Yeah. Kind of."

"Is she mad at me?"

"Would she have hugged you if she was mad at you?"

I hadn't thought of it that way.

"She's not mad at you Ashlee. She understands why you and Ryan killed her. She's sorry she tried to expose you. And she's sorry she didn't tell you she was a werewolf."

I nodded.

"She wants you to answer a question." Cole said suddenly.

"What is it?" I asked.

"She wants to know if, after I bring her back, would you be her friend again?"

I turned toward the shimmer. "You know I'll say yes. Why do you even ask?"

I held out my arms and the shimmer flew into them. It was awkward to hug a ghost. It was kind of like hugging air, but kind of like hugging an invisible person.

I backed up and Karla let go. I turned to Cole, who was about to fall. I caught him and let him lean on me again.

"When are you going to bring her back?" I asked.

"In a few hours. I need to rest awhile." he answered sleepily.

"Do you want me to have Grace get the car and take you back to her place?"

He nodded.

I looked around and found Grace standing over Duke. I called her over. She came unwillingly.

"What do you need?" she asked.

"Can you go get your car and take Cole back to the house?" I asked.

She looked at him and her eyes widened. "What's wrong with him?"

"He's tired because of all the necromancy he had to do. Can you take him back to the house?"

She nodded and ran off to get the car.

"We should have all the injured go to the house with her too." I said.

"That would be a good idea. If only Grace had a bigger car." Cole said.

"Right. How's that broken arm treating you?"

"It's pretty painful. Ryan told me you set it and made the splint."

"Yeah, I did."

"Thanks. But now you are walking around with one shoe."

"So?"

"You don't care. I know. But I don't think it's safe to walk around this field without a shoe."

"Don't worry. I've been watching the ground to make sure I don't step on anything."

He shrugged.

Grace walked over to us.

"You brought your Mustang, right?" I asked.

"Yes."

"I guess we could squeeze the injured in it."

"You won't have to."

"What do you mean?"

"I had Dwayne turn it into a van."

"Oh. Isn't that James's dad?"

"Yeah."

"It's weird that James has black hair with silver at the ends but Dwayne has auburn hair.

And James has blue eyes but Dwayne has black eyes. Otherwise they look the same."

"James got his hair and his eyes from his mother. The rest was from his dad."

"Yeah. That makes sense. Where is his mom?"

"Dead."

I looked at James. He was laughing even though he had a broken leg and a wrapped up head. I looked back at my sister.

"He didn't know her. She died giving birth to him." she explained.

I nodded.

"Come on," I said, "Let's get the injured into your *van.*"

She glared at me then laughed. She had sworn to me that she would never get a van.

Grace went over to tell the injured they needed to get in the van so she could drive them to the house. Then she helped someone who was lying on the ground. Duke. She helped him up and walked him to the van. The other injured followed her.

I walked Cole over to the van still supporting his weight. I helped him into the van as Ryan walked up. Cole thanked me.

"Do you have a list now?" I asked Ryan.

"Yeah. Get in the van. I'll meet you at the house." he answered.

He leaned down and kissed me on the cheek. Then he ran off to help the others with the dead bodies.

Grace pulled onto the road and drove away from the battle ground. I looked at the sky. It was dark.

"Grace. What time is it?" I asked.

"Ten thirty-five. Time for you to stop worrying about every little detail. Go to sleep or something."

I was sitting by Cole. He was already asleep against the window. I leaned back in the seat and closed my eyes.

* * *

"Hey, Ashlee. Wake up." I heard Cole say.

Someone shook my shoulder. I opened my eyes.

I was lying against Cole's shoulder. No one had shaken me, it was the road. I sat up rubbing my eyes.

"Sorry. That was your broken arm wasn't it?" I said.

"Yeah. It's okay. You needed sleep. I woke you up because we are almost to the house."

I nodded.

We passed the school as he told me.

When we got to the last house on the street Grace pulled up to the front curb. She got out and opened the back door for everyone. Cole and I waited for everyone else to get out then I got out and helped him.

Everyone was already in the house by the time I closed the door. When I did the van turned back to a Mustang. I helped Cole up the walk and into the house. Then I took him upstairs to the boys' room. He thanked me as I left.

I walked back down to the living room. When I walked in I saw Duke and John on the couch. Paul was in the recliner and James was sitting in the floor, his broken leg stretched out.

Duke had casts on his left arm, left leg, and his right wrist. His face was bruised up and he looked like he'd been bitten a hundred times.

James just had a broken leg. He seemed fine. He didn't even pay attention to the cast.

Paul's head was wrapped and his left foot was in a splint. He looked tired. He was staring at the kitchen door, probably waiting for a meal.

John had both of his legs in casts. I wondered how he'd broken them. I remembered seeing him, in human form, jumping out of a tree to land on a vampire's back. That was probably when he broke his legs.

My sister came through the door with two trays in her hands. Dwayne came in behind her also carrying two trays. The trays had been piled with food. They handed them out to the injured boys.

"Ashlee, do you mind taking Cole's up to him?" Grace asked me.

I nodded and got the tray from the kitchen. I went upstairs to Ryan, Cole, and Duke's room. I knocked then opened the door.

Cole was awake. I laid the tray across his lap and he thanked me through a mouthful of food.

"I think, after I'm done eating, I'll be strong enough to bring Karla back." Cole told me.

"You don't have to rush yourself. Karla is very patient." I nodded to the shimmer.

"I know. But I'm going to do it as soon as I'm done eating."

"Okay. If you think you can."

I turned to walk out the door.

"Wait." Cole said.

I turned back to him.

"I might need your help." he confessed.

"I'm not a necromancer. You know that."

"Yeah. But you were close to Karla. Do you have anything of hers?"

"Yeah. Well, it was hers but she gave it to me."

"That'll work. Can you bring it here?"

I reached down to my ankle and unclasped the anklet that Karla had traded to me. I handed it to Cole. He looked it over.

"Can you get me a bowl and a lighter?" he asked.

I looked around the room. There was a bowl on the dresser. I picked it up and tossed it to him. Then I walked over to Ryan's bed and reached under his pillow. I grabbed the lighter and handed it to Cole. He looked behind me at Ryan's bed. He didn't know his brother slept with that stuff. He looked back down at the stuff I gave him.

"Okay. Don't freak out." he told me.

I nodded.

He dropped the anklet into the bowl.

"What was her favorite flower?" he asked.

"Roses."

"Get me some rose petals."

I walked into the boys' bathroom and came out with a handful of rose petals. Cole raised his eyebrows but didn't say anything. He motioned for me to drop the petals in the bowl. I did.

"Did she wear the same size clothes as you?" he asked

I nodded.

"Go get some clothes. When she comes back she won't have any." he told me.

I went to Mikayla's room and grabbed a pair of my pants and a shirt. I went to Mikayla's closet and got a jacket. Then I went back to Cole and laid the clothes on Ryan's bed.

"Okay. This is the part I need you not to freak out about." he said.

He lit the lighter and lowered it into the bowl full of rose petals and the anklet. The rose petals caught on fire. Cole stood and put the bowl in the middle of the floor. The shimmer moved to stand over the bowl. Cole shut his eyes as Karla started to materialize. He was mumbling but I didn't understand what he was saying, he was speaking some other language.

Karla was solid now but I knew the process wasn't done. She was glowing. Her skin was twitching. Then, all of a sudden, she stopped glowing and twitching and fell to the floor beside the bowl. The fire had gone out.

I grabbed the clothes and ran up to her. She tried to push herself to her knees but her arms weren't strong enough. I helped her up. She smiled at me and held her arms over her head for me to put the shirt on. I stood and pulled the shirt over her head. I helped her stand up and put the pants on. She wanted to put the jacket on by herself but she put it on upside down and I had to help her anyway. She reached down in the bowl and lifted the anklet out of the charred rose petals. It wasn't damaged at all.

She handed it to me. I bent down to put it on her ankle but she moved her foot away. I looked up at her and she pointed to my ankle. I shook my head.

"I want you to have it." I told her.

She shrugged and gave me her ankle. I clasped the anklet and stood. I turned to Cole. His eyes were still shut.

"She's dressed Cole. You can look now." I told him.

The opened his eyes.

"How do you like it?" he asked Karla.

"I like it a lot." she answered smiling.

She sounded exactly the same as she used to. She looked exactly the same too. Nothing had changed.

"And you aren't a werewolf anymore. Or a ghost. Or a human." Cole told her.

"Then what am I?"

"You are a reborn spirit."

"So if I am talking to a supernatural and they ask what I am I just say, 'oh, yeah. I'm just a spirit. You know. I was reborn.'"

"Yeah. You have to include 'reborn' because you aren't just a spirit anymore. You have come back."

"What's a shorter term for that?"

"A necromantic."

"I'll say that then."

I laughed at her and she smiled at me. My stomach growled and Karla laughed at me.

"You hungry necromantic?" I asked her.

"Actually, now that you mention it, I am." she frowned.

"Let's get you something to eat then."

"Shouldn't you change out of your bloody clothes?"

"Is the Queen coming to eat with us?" I asked.

She laughed and rolled her eyes at me.

"Is it possible that you've gotten even more immature?" she asked me.

"Hey. I am *very* mature!" I laughed.

"And I really think you guys should go eat." Cole said.

We looked at him. He looked like he was going to pass out. Just as he started to fall I caught him. I walked him over to his bed. He laid down.

"I told you that you should have waited." I said.

"I'm fine. Just tired." he told me.

He rolled over and went to sleep.

Karla and I walked out the door. I closed it behind us. Then I heard voices. Something was going on down stairs. I listened to two voices I didn't know. Then I heard my sister and Ryan. They were arguing with the other two voices. I listened closer.

"They are needed for questioning." a guy I didn't know.

"Why would a girl kill her best friend?" Grace.

"There are many reasons. Such as fighting over a boy." a woman I didn't know.

"Ashlee loved Karla. She would never have killed her. And being Ashlee's boyfriend, I wouldn't kill someone she loved." Ryan.

I motioned for Karla to go into the room beside us. She ran in and I went down stairs.

The two people, whose voices I hadn't recognized, were cops. They were in uniform and they were staring me down. I tried to look as helpless as possible. Wasn't hard.

I walked over to Ryan and he put his arm around my shoulders.

The woman cop looked me over.

"What's the silver stuff on your clothes?" she asked.

"Paint. I was painting my sister's room." I answered.

"Why's your shirt ripped?"

"I needed to use part of it as a rag."

"Where's your other shoe?"

"I was taking my shoes off when I heard voices."

"Why didn't you put your shoe back on to come down here?"

"It would have taken too long."

She glared at me. I had an answer for anything she asked.

The man stepped in.

"Hello. My name is Officer Maiming. This is my partner, Officer Cloven. We would like to ask a few questions about your friend Karla."

"I would be happy to answer them. Will it help you find out who killed her?"

"That's what we are hoping, young lady."

I nodded.

"Are you ready?" Officer Maiming asked.

"Yes." I answered in a small voice.

"Where were you the night Karla Case was killed?"

"At my house."

"Was your boyfriend with you?"

"Yes."

"Why was he with you?"

"He had just moved to town so I had asked him to come over for dinner."

"Now, is it true that both you and Karla had ladders by your windows?"

"Yes sir."

"Why is that?"

"So we could easily visit each other."

"Could you elaborate?"

"When one of us was sick we would go to each other's windows. Sir."

"People that you go to school with said you got in a fight with Karla the day of her death. Is that true?"

"Yes, it is."

"Would you explain what the fight was about?"

"I don't really remember. We would fight over a lot of stupid things."

"Could you try to remember for us?"

I looked over at the woman. She'd been quietly writing down my answers the whole time. I tilted my head to the side then looked back at Officer Maiming.

"I think we were fighting about an anklet." I said.

"Could you show me this anklet?" Officer Maiming asked.

"No. I don't have it anymore."

"Where is it?"

"It was buried with Karla."

"Why were you two fighting over it?"

"She and I traded a lot of things. She traded me her anklet for my necklace. She wanted the anklet back because she broke the clasp on the necklace. And we argued about it."

"Why did you let her be buried with the anklet?"

"I felt bad that we fought over it."

Officer Maiming looked at Officer Cloven. She nodded.

"Thank you Ashlee. We've already questioned your family, your boyfriend, and Karla's family. We will get back to you." Officer Maiming told me.

"Do you think you could find out who killed my friend?" I asked, tears filled my eyes.

Officer Maiming patted my shoulder. "We'll try our best."

We thanked them then they got in their car and drove away.

"Nice save Ash." Ryan said.

"Thanks. I'll go get Karla now." I started up the stairs but Ryan grabbed my arm.

"Ashlee, Karla is dead. You can't go get her." he said frowning.

"No. She's up in James's room."

Ryan let go of my arm. He looked worried but walked over to Duke and sat down beside him.

I ran upstairs and got Karla out of James's room. She followed me downstairs and we stopped in the living room.

Ryan jumped to his feet. His face got deathly pale. He stared at Karla and pointed.

"Ryan. It's rude to point." I said.

He put his hand down but continued to stare.

"How the heck is she here? And alive?" he blurted out.

"Your brother brought her back. By the way, he is extremely tired. So don't bother him." I answered and advised.

"What?"

"You heard me." I told him, I turned to Karla, "Come on Karla. Let's find something to eat."

She followed me into the kitchen. I went straight to the freezer and got out a steak. I put it on a plate and let it thaw. I turned to Karla.

"What do you want?" I asked.

"What are you having?"

"A bloody steak. I don't think you'd want that though."

She crinkled her nose.

"What else is there?" she asked.

"Want some cereal?"

"That works."

I got her a bowl of cereal and took it to the table for her. She sat down and ate it happily.

When my steak had thawed enough I put it in the microwave for a minute. I know you aren't supposed to put steak in a microwave but it didn't take as long so I didn't care.

I got my steak out. Blood was spreading across the plate. I sat down across from Karla at the table. She looked up as I cut the steak into squares and put one to my mouth. She probably thought I was going to eat it because when bit into it and sucked the blood out she gasped. I dropped the shriveled meat square on the plate. I looked up at her. She was staring at the bloodless square.

I quickly finished my steak and took my plate to the sink.

"Are you done with that bowl?" I asked Karla.

"Yeah." she brought it in and put it in the sink with my plate.

I walked out of the kitchen and Karla followed me. I went upstairs to Cole's room to grab his sword but it wasn't there. I tried to remember what he had done with it. He had left it in Grace's car.

I felt the waist band of my jeans. The silver dagger I had taken from Jafar was there. I didn't really remember putting it there but it seemed like the place I would put something.

I pulled it out. The silver blade had dried silver blood on it. I would have to chip the blood off. I turned and Karla squeaked. She was staring at the dagger.

"Sorry. I didn't mean to scare you." I apologized.

I walked around her and back downstairs. She followed. I stopped in the living room. I saw James sitting in the corner of the couch. I walked over to him. He looked up and smiled.

"Hey Ash. Need something?" he asked.

He looked eager to do anything.

"I just wanted to know if you had fixed those dummies." I said.

"Yeah. I fixed them for Cole to practice before the fight but he didn't use them. They're out in the yard."

I thanked him and started toward the kitchen. Ryan walked up to me.

"Can I go out there with you?" he asked.

"Yeah." I answered.

We walked through the kitchen and out the back door. I walked straight toward the dummies. Their swords were stuck in the ground beside them and they were just relaxing against the fence. When they saw me they picked up their swords and stood.

"Just one of you, for now." I said.

I pointed my dagger at the taller one. The other one went back to the fence.

"Before you start practicing could I talk to you?" Ryan asked.

"Hold on a second." I told the dummy. He gave me a thumbs up and sat down right where he was.

I turned to Ryan.

"I have the list of survivors." he told me.

"Read it to me." I said.

He looked down at the paper.

"Cole, Grace, Duke, Dwayne, James, Mikayla, Stefan, John, Paul, Lynette, Sandy, Tyler, Mr. Watson, and Jimmy."

"Who all is injured?"

"Everyone but you."

"Fine. Who is extremely injured?"

"Cole, Duke, James, Paul, and John."

"And how are they healing?"

"I checked on Cole and he's healing like a human. James seems not to notice. Paul and John show that they are in pain but they are healing fast. And Duke is . . . well, he's healing slower than werewolves usually do, but he is okay."

"That's good."

He nodded.

"Why is Ashlee the only one who isn't injured?" Karla asked.

"She has the gene. She's a fighter and it's in her blood." Ryan answered.

"Oh."

I walked over to the dummy. He stood and bowed to me. I nodded and he stood straight. I started fighting him.

CHAPTER 19
The Thing in the Shadows

Dwayne, James, Paul, John, Lynette, Sandy, Tyler, and Mr. Watson had gone home as soon as they were well enough. Grace had made breakfast for the people who had stayed.

We sat around the living room. There were only eight of us left. Cole, Ryan, Grace, Duke, Mikayla, Stefan, Jimmy, and me. Well, nine if you count Karla. I didn't count her as she really had nowhere else to go.

Mikayla and Stefan were planning on staying with Grace for a while. Jimmy said he would probably stay with her too. Ryan wanted to keep Cole here until he was stronger and his arm was a little better. Duke was going to stay until he was done healing so he didn't scare mom. I would stay there with Duke.

Ryan stood up and motioned for me to follow him. He walked through the kitchen and out the back door. I followed him. He dropped into one of the lawn chairs and I sat in the one beside him. He held my hand in the space between us.

"I'm sorry. You probably feel bad about all those people dying for us." Ryan said.

"Fifteen people. Plus, in the end, Jafar begged me to kill her because Alexander had admitted that he had used her." I said.

"I *really* am sorry. I know you didn't want this."

"As long as you are alive I'm okay."

"And as long as you are so am I."

I looked over at him. He was smiling at the sky. I could have lost him. He could have died in the fight and I didn't really think about it until now.

"If you would have died I wouldn't wait around to die a natural death. I would die with you. I would have let them kill me." I told him.

He looked over at me. "I want to say I'm disappointed in you but I can't. I would have done the same thing."

"Well, what if you *thought* I died but I really didn't? Then you killed yourself and I didn't know and someone told me they thought you had run away. And Cole died so I couldn't ask him to help me find you and you wouldn't be able to tell him to tell me that you didn't run away but you had died. What would you do in that situation?"

"Well, I would write you a very long message in the dirt explaining everything. After I write the note what would you do?"

"Get in a fight that I know I can't win. Then I'd get killed and I would be with you again."

We laughed.

"We have the weirdest conversations." Ryan said.

I nodded. We stopped laughing at the same time.

"I love you." Ryan said.

"I love you too."

We looked up at the sky and watched the clouds roll by. We told each other when we saw figures formed in the clouds. We laughed and held hands. That's when Cole ran out the backdoor.

"The cops called," he said, "They have their suspect. It's neither of you but they want you to come in and see if you recognize the person."

Ryan and I looked at each other. We were thinking the same thing. How could they have a suspect if *we* were the ones that had killed Karla?

We got up and went into the house. Grace was waiting for us. She said she was going too, whether the police liked it or not. She drove us over to the police station.

*   *   *

We walked up to the counter. The man behind it asked our names and sent us down a long hallway with one room at the end. Grace didn't even knock on the door, she just busted right in. Ryan and I followed.

The two cops that had been at Grace's house were there. Along with another cop who looked older than them. I read his badge: Sheriff. I was not about to make this guy mad, but Grace would if need be.

The sheriff nodded to us to sit in the two chairs across from him. Grace pushed Ryan and me toward the chairs. We sat down and Grace moved behind me, putting her hands on my shoulders.

"So Officer Maiming here tells me that you wanted him to let you know if we found anything, is that correct?" the sheriff said slowly, as if I were a child.

"Yes sir." I answered.

"Well, everyone's story seems to match up. That leaves us with one suspect. One man who has been chased all over the country. Alexander Gazpacho. Do you recognize the name?"

"No sir."

"Are you sure? Do you think Karla would have known the name?"

"She did tell me about someone named Alex. She said she met them online and they were really weird so she deleted him."

"Did she ever tell you the full name?"

"No sir. I thought we were done being questioned. I don't really enjoy talking about this."

"Of course. Do you have any questions for me?"

"One."

"Go ahead."

"Do you really think it was a vampire who killed my friend?"

The cops laughed.

"No. That's just something the press says." Officer Maiming answered, "We have nothing to do with that."

"Then why was the saliva like a leech's but also like a human's?"

"It was nothing like a human's dear. It was all leech. That's how Alexander kills his victims. Giant leeches."

I nodded.

"Any other questions dear?" Officer Cloven asked.

"Yes. Will you be going after this Alexander now?" I asked.

"Yes, we will. And we will get him. You have nothing to worry about."

She smiled at me and I wondered, what happened to being the bad cop?

"That is all we can release to you." the sheriff said.

"You want us to leave now?" I asked.

He nodded.

We stood and left the room. As soon as we were out the door Grace started rambling.

"They should be able to tell us more. They were lying through their teeth. I can't believe those people. And officer what's-her-face was oddly nice this time. What got up her-?"

"Grace! Stop babbling." I said closing my eyes.

"Sorry." she mumbled.

Ryan put his arm over my shoulders. I opened my eyes and looked up at him.

"They weren't lying." I said.

"I know." he whispered.

"They really think it was Alex and that he used giant leeches. That's the only thing that sounds stupid."

"Yeah. It makes no sense. Sometimes it's better to let humans make assumptions and just go with whatever they say. They don't want to believe that we exist."

We walked out of the police office and got into Grace's Mustang. I sat in the passenger seat staring out the window. We were approaching the school when I saw something in the tree line. I had to do a double-take to make sure it wasn't just my eyes.

"Stop the car." I said calmly.

Grace still slammed on the brakes and almost sent me through the windshield.

I got out of the car, Ryan right behind me. I searched the tree line for the shadow figure. I found it but it dissolved as soon as I looked in its direction.

"What was that?" Ryan asked.

"I don't know. I doubt it's anything good though." I said.

I walked back to the car and let Ryan in before me. He crawled in the backseat. As I watched him I saw something shinny. Cole's sword. I climbed in the front seat.

"Don't forget to take your brother's sword in the house." I told Ryan.

He mumbled something that I didn't catch. I saw light glance off the sword as he picked it up.

We pulled into the driveway and got out of the car quickly. On my way to the door I looked over my shoulder. I saw a bush across the street, it looked like the wind was moving it. There was no wind. I looked closer and saw the shadow figure. Again, as soon as I made eye-contact, it dissolved.

I ran in the house and slammed the door behind me.

"What's wrong?" Ryan asked.

"That thing we saw earlier was in a bush across the street."

"Did you see what it was?"

"No. All I can see is a dark figure. As soon as I look at it, it dissolves."

Everyone in the house looked at me.

"Dissolves?" Mikayla asked, probably thinking she heard wrong.

"Yes. Dissolves." I answered.

"Ashlee, no living thing can just 'dissolve,' you know that."

"Maybe it's not a *normal* living thing. *Normal* vampires can't read minds but Ryan and I can. That sounds almost the same to me."

"I highly doubt that the thing you saw dissolved. Maybe it moved too fast for you to see."

"Vampire vision. Nothing moves too fast for me to see."

"Then maybe you are just seeing things. You've been under a lot of stress. It's probably getting to you."

"I'm not crazy, Mikayla. Ryan saw it too."

Mikayla looked at Ryan.

"I did. And it did look to me like it dissolved." he said.

"You've been under a lot of stress too. You guys are probably just seeing things." Mikayla said shaking her head.

"How did we see the same exact thing?" I asked.

Mikayla's eyebrows knitted together. She chewed on her bottom lip. She didn't know how to answer.

"Mikayla. The thing dissolved. I'll do some research. There has to be something going on." I told her.

She nodded.

"I'm going to use your laptop." I said.

She nodded again.

I ran up stairs to the room I was sharing with Mikayla. The colors on everything were still disorienting. I grabbed her laptop and went back downstairs then sat down in the middle of the floor.

"Look up something called the 'shadow traveler' or anything to do with shadows." Mikayla said.

I typed 'shadow traveler' in the search box. There was only one result. I clicked on it. A picture of a tree line was at the top of the screen. I saw a dark figure in it. As I watched, it dissolved then reappeared somewhere else in the picture.

"It's a shadow traveler." I said.

Everyone looked at me. Ryan got up and stood on his knees behind me. He looked confused.

"Um. What's a shadow traveler?" Karla asked.

I read the description:

"Shadow travelers stay in the shadows, they can't leave them. Appears as a dark figure. They travel by shadow. Appear to dissolve into the shadows when they are trying to travel. In times of war they are used as spies. They can't enter a person's dwelling, whether it's human or supernatural."

"So it can't get in here?"

"No. This is a dwelling. Wherever people live, they can't go."

"That makes me feel loads better." she sighed.

Ryan shifted his weight behind me.

"This doesn't make sense." he said.

"What doesn't? Alexander is using shadow travelers to see if we are building another army." I said.

"No, not that. That made perfect sense. What doesn't make sense is that the shadow travelers are supposed to be extinct."

"What do you mean 'supposed to be'?"

"Well, they were supposed to have become extinct at least twenty-five years ago. Obviously, that one wasn't extinct. I've never even seen one before now. So either, they never *truly* were extinct or Cole brought them back."

Everyone glanced at Cole.

"Whoa. Wait a second. How did *I* bring them back?" Cole asked shocked.

"When you raised the dead you could have raised other things along with it. And since the shadow travelers never really had a solid body they just went back to their true form." Ryan explained.

"And you have *never* seen one of these things until now? After I raised the dead?"

"Never."

Cole looked at me. I shook my head.

"Look and see what happened to them." he said pointing at the computer.

I looked through the whole page and finally found it at the end. I read it to Cole:

"The shadow travelers are now extinct. You can't see them anywhere. Only a very powerful necromancer could bring them back. The necromancers are also extinct."

"What? Am I the only necromancer in existence then?" Cole asked. He was panicking.

"I guess. On the plus side, you're really powerful." Ryan said to him.

"How is that a plus side?"

"Power is key in the supernatural world."

I felt everyone quickly look at me then away.

CHAPTER 20
Struggling and Planning

"Ashlee, you have to get out of the house. Or at least out of bed." Ryan said.

I was under the covers on my air mattress. I'd been here all day after we found out about the shadow travelers. Grace had sent Ryan to get me out of my bed at least five times now.

"Go away." I grumbled into the mattress.

"I'm not going anywhere." Ryan promised.

"And I'm not getting up."

"You will if I drag you out of there."

"If you do I will punch you."

"No, you won't."

"Probably not. But I would go find somewhere else to hide. So either way it won't work."

He grabbed my ankles under the covers and tried to pull me off the mattress. I grabbed the mattress so he was just pulling me around on it. He sighed.

"You have to come out." he said.

"No. I don't. And I won't." I told him.

He tried to yank the covers back but I had hold of them and it didn't work. He growled.

"Come on! Just get up!" he begged.

"No!"

This time he put his arms around my waist and picked me up then threw me over his shoulder. I was screaming and punching his back the whole time. The covers had fallen off my head so I could see that he was taking me downstairs.

He walked in the living room and put me on the couch. I threw the covers back over my head and curled into a ball.

"Well, at least you're not upstairs anymore." Ryan said.

"Leave me alone." I growled at him.

"Just take the covers off!"

"No!"

"Why are you being such a child?"

"Because I am one."

"No, you're not."

"I am a normal kid who wants to stay in bed."

He sighed.

He knew I wanted to be normal. He knew that I didn't want to have the gene and be the one in the prophecy. He also knew that he couldn't give me that.

"Will you eat something?" he asked. "You haven't eaten all day. You need food."

"No. I don't want food." I said.

I truly wasn't hungry. I had lost my appetite when we found out that we had helped our only enemy.

"Please? For me?" he said sweetly.

"No. That doesn't work on me and you know it."

"Ashlee," Duke said, "You do need to eat something. Please eat. For me?"

"Fine." I growled.

"She'll eat for you but not me." Ryan whispered.

"I'm not moving though." I told them.

"You don't have to." Ryan told me.

"Good."

Then I realized what he had meant. He picked me up and threw me over his shoulder again. This time I was so wrapped up in the covers that I felt like I was being straggled.

"Really Ryan!" I growled.

"Yes, really." he said laughing.

I tried to hit him but the covers were too tight for me to move. He sat me down in a chair somewhere but I didn't know where we were. I tried to find a way out of the covers. I couldn't find one.

"Um, Ryan." I said, "A little help please."

I heard him chuckle then walk over to me. He worked with the covers. Unfolding and unwrapping until he finally got me out, except for my legs. They were still trapped in the covers. He probably left me like that so I couldn't run away.

Now that I was out, I realized we were in the kitchen. He was getting something out of the freezer. I thought it was another steak until he put it in a cup. He stuck it in the microwave then walked over to the cabinets and got a box of cereal. The milk was already on the counter so he fixed me a bowl.

He walked toward me with the bowl but the microwave beeped. He got the cup out and came over to me. I pushed out the chair beside me for him to sit in. He put the bowl and cup in front of me.

I was curious about the cup so I picked it up first. In it was warm blood. It was steaming from the time in the microwave.

"What kind of blood is this?" I asked.

"Animal blood. All the excess from the steaks we had." he answered.

I drank some of it. It tasted amazing. I finished it in no time. Then I ate my cereal slowly. Ryan knew I didn't like cereal so he didn't argue much when I didn't finish it. Seeing as that's all Grace had, I had to at least eat some of it. When I was done Ryan looked up and laughed at me.

"What?" I asked offended.

"Hold on."

He got up and walked to the sink. He came back with a washcloth. I held out my hand but he just sat down in his chair. I looked at him with my eyebrows raised. He gestured for me to come sit on his lap. I shook my head but did as he said. Or tried to. I almost fell because my legs were still wrapped up. He caught me and sat me down on his lap.

He wiped my mouth and chin then showed me the washcloth. There was a lot of blood on it. Apparently I was a messy eater. After my face was clean he untangled my legs, which was harder than freeing my arms and head. He laughed at me as I glared down at the covers.

"It's your own fault, you know?" he said, "If you wouldn't have twisted your blankets up this would have been easier."

"It wasn't my fault. It was yours." I corrected.

"How was it mine?"

"You had to drag me out of my bed, throw me over your shoulder, put me on the couch, and then throw me over your shoulder again."

"Okay. It's partially my fault. But some of it's yours for not getting up."

"Fair enough."

He worked with the covers until he finally got them untangled. He threw them into the corner of the room then wrapped his arms around my waist. I leaned back into his chest.

Grace walked in the door and straight to the fridge. She glanced in our direction and did a double-take. She stared at us for a few seconds. Then she continued whatever she was doing.

"Hey guys." she said as she was pawing through the fridge.

"Hey." I said.

"Hi Grace." Ryan muttered into my hair.

"Why don't you guys come out to the living room now that Ashlee is up?" Grace asked.

She grabbed a bowl full of red stuff. It wasn't blood. It looked like something Cole would use for necromancy. That's exactly what it was for.

Grace walked into the living room. Ryan and I looked at each other then got up and followed her.

When we walked in the room everyone looked up. Duke tried to get up so I could sit with him on the couch but I held up my hand. He sighed and fell back down. I walked over to the other couch and sat down beside Mikayla. She smiled and hugged me around the shoulders. Stefan smiled and nodded at me.

Jimmy just stared at the window. That told me that everyone was just trying to make me feel better, but Jimmy knew it wouldn't work so he didn't try. That's the good thing about having a twin.

"You guys don't have to make me feel better." I told them, "And I know that's what you are trying to do."

They all looked at each other then back at me.

"Jimmy said it wouldn't work. Which is why he's not trying." Mikayla said.

"I know. He's my twin. Remember?"

"Oh. Right. Well, we want to help you. You seem so depressed and we are worried about you."

"I'm not depressed."

"Oh really?"

Sarcasm. Fantastic.

"I'm seriously not depressed." I said slowly, "I just want to be normal and I never will be. So I'm just a little sensitive right now."

"I'm really sorry about that." Mikayla said seriously.

"It's fine. Honestly. Either way, I realize I need to focus."

"On what?"

"Alexander."

"The fight is over. You don't have to worry about that anymore."

"The fight is over *for now*. Alexander got away. He's building another army. There will be a second fight."

Everyone was staring at me with their mouths open, except for Jimmy. He just stared out the window. Everyone else closed their mouths and started talking again.

"So . . . Ashlee," Ryan said hesitantly, "do you want to go upstairs and discuss wedding details?"

I nodded.

We stood and went upstairs. The others started talking quietly as soon as we left the room. They were talking about me and my genes. I tuned them out.

Ryan and I walked into his room and closed the door. It surprised me that Cole wasn't there. Ryan jumped onto his bed. I walked over and lay sideways at the foot of it. He grabbed a pad of paper and a pen from the bed side table and handed them to me. I took them and started writing out sections.

"You're already writing?" Ryan asked, eyebrows raised.

"I'm just writing headings: bride's maids, best man, ushers, flower girl, ring bearer, etcetera."

"Oh. So who's going to fill those roles?"

"I don't know about your ushers and best man. But Mikayla is going to be my maid of honor. My bride's maids are going to be Grace, Lynette, and Sandy."

"Can there be two best men?"

"I don't think so."

"Well, I'm going to have two."

"Um. Okay. Who?"

"Cole and Duke."

"And your ushers?"

"Stefan and Jimmy."

I wrote all the names down.

"What about the flower girl and ring bearer?" Ryan asked.

I looked up. I had someone in mind for flower girl but I was sure that Ryan wouldn't like it.

"Who?" he sighed.

He'd been reading my mind.

"Karla." I told him.

"You know she can't. She's supposed to be dead."

"She could have a disguise."

"Okay. Karla will be our flower girl."

I smiled and wrote her name down.

"Ring bearer?" I asked him.

"I think it should be James."

I nodded and wrote him down.

"Where are we going to have the ceremony and where are we going to have the reception?" I asked.

"We could have the ceremony in Grace's giant backyard."

"And the reception in my parents' backyard?"

"That works."

I wrote the venues on the margin of the paper. Then I wrote the word flowers on one of the lines. I looked up at Ryan.

"Flowers?" I asked.

"That I can't help with."

"Roses, lilacs, orange blossom, tiger lilies, morning glories, cherry blossom, and stargazer lilies?"

"Sure? I have no clue what any of those look like except for the roses."

I laughed and wrote the list of flowers.

"In my bouquet I want roses, tiger lilies, morning glories, stargazer lilies, and fern leaves." I said.

"Okay."

He had no idea what I was talking about. I just wrote them down and moved on.

"Something old, something new, something borrowed, and something blue." I said absently.

"What?" Ryan said confused.

I looked up.

"Don't worry about it. It's just bride stuff." I told him.

He shrugged.

"That's basically all we need." I said.

"What about dresses and tuxes?"

"Don't worry about that stuff. I got it taken care of."

"Okay then."

"What colors do you want at the wedding?"

"I'm guessing you want black and red. Even though black shouldn't be used at a wedding."

"Yeah."

"So, I guess, just use black and red."

"Yes!"

He laughed.

"We need six tuxes and five dresses. Beside your tux and my dress." I said.

We were done. I kept worrying Alex would ruin the wedding.

CHAPTER 21
The Truth

I t was a week after the fight when Cole and Duke were finally well enough to return home. Grace gave Ryan and Cole a ride home then came back and waited for Duke and me. She also told me that the red stuff in the bowl was something that a necromancer can eat to make them stronger faster.

Duke had to take a shower and I had to change out of my bloody clothes. Mikayla gave me one of her outfits to wear. When I walked out of Mikayla's room I almost ran into Jimmy.

"Sorry, Jimmy. I wasn't paying attention." I told him.

"It's okay." he laughed.

"Thanks for not trying to cheer me up all week like the rest of them."

"I knew it wouldn't help. I also thought it might irritate you."

"Yeah. It did actually."

"I could tell."

"Oh, have I told you that Ryan wants you to be one of his ushers?"

"You haven't. But okay."

"So you'll do it?"

"Of course. When is the wedding anyway?"

"Some time after we graduate. Probably in June."

"Sounds good."

I nodded.

The bathroom door opened and Duke limped out. It was a small limp a human wouldn't notice, unless that human was my mother. We planned to tell her that Duke stepped in a hole in the backyard.

"Hey. You and Grace ready?" Duke asked while drying his hair.

"Yeah. Just waiting for you." I said.

"I'm ready now."

He threw the towel over his shoulder and into the laundry basket by the bathroom door. I smiled at him.

We left Jimmy with hurried good-byes. Duke limped down the stairs in front of me. He tripped on the last step but Grace caught him. She had been waiting at the foot of the stairs. She helped him regain his balance then motioned for us to go ahead of her. We walked around her and out the door.

My eyes went directly to the bush across the street. There I saw another shadow traveler. Earlier, when Grace had taken Cole and Ryan home, I had seen two. They had followed Grace's car.

I got in the backseat as Duke protested. Although he had a healing broken leg that no longer needed a cast, he still thought of others before himself. Something I loved about my half-brother.

Grace walked out and got in the car without saying a word. She had been freaking out over the shadow travelers all day. I could see that she was still nervous.

"Mom will ask why you're limping." She said as she pulled away from the curb.

"I know. Ashlee already came up with a fake reason. Remember, you were there." Duke sighed.

She nodded.

The rest of the ride was silent. I watched out the window as we passed by the school, the library, YMCA, Wal-Mart, and the park. Then I watched as we passed the distantly familiar houses of my neighborhood.

Grace stopped right in front of our house. She got out to let me out then got right back in. She wasn't staying to visit our parents. I walked around the car and helped Duke get out. As soon as I turned to walk up the sidewalk I practically got tackled by my mother (Step mom, aunt, whatever). My dad was smiling behind her. I hugged her back.

"Hi . . . Mom." I said confused.

I knew I still had to call her mom because she didn't know. It sounded awkward to call her that now that I knew she wasn't my birth mother. But she was still my mom. If that made sense.

"Hi honey!" She squealed.

Duke started to walk toward the house. My mom looked over at him

"Adam? Why are you limping?" she asked him.

"Oh. I stepped in a hole in Grace's backyard. I'm fine though." he answered.

She hugged him tightly. He was at least five inches taller than her now. She let go and looked up at him.

"You've gotten tall." she exclaimed.

I laughed then looked at my dad.

When I looked at him his expression became serious. He cleared his throat and my mom looked at him over her shoulder.

"I'm going to take a walk with my daughter." he told her.

"Alright." she said.

She helped Duke into the house. Grace had already left.

My dad started walking toward the park. I had no choice but to follow. I wanted answers. He should give them to me. Jimmy had called him at Grace's house and he knew that I had met my twin. I could tell he didn't like it much.

My dad walked all the way to the park and stopped at the gates. He turned to face me.

"Go ahead. Ask." he said.

"Here?" I asked.

"Yes. Ask me."

"Okay. Why didn't you tell me?"

"You didn't need to know."

"Didn't need to know that my life is a *lie*? That the person I thought was my mother is really my *aunt*? That Grace and Duke are my half siblings *and* my cousins?"

"I didn't think it was necessary for you to worry about at the time. I was waiting until you were older."

"Tell me the whole story."

He sighed and pinched the bridge of his nose. Then he looked me straight in the face and told me the truth.

"I was with your birth mother before I met your aunt and fell in love with her. Thing is, your mother was expecting you and Jimmy. I married your aunt when your mother was only a month into the pregnancy. She didn't tell me she was pregnant until two days after the wedding. I had one of my witch friends perform a spell on my wife that would make her go through the stages of pregnancy without actually having a baby. The time came that your mother was going into labor. I knocked out my wife with a potion the witch had given me. She was expecting only one child, when I got to the hospital and saw two children; I knew I had to hide one of you. My wife always wanted a girl, so I brought you home. Your mother died an hour after giving birth so I couldn't leave Jimmy with her. It took me three hours to get you two out of the hospital. Another hour to hide Jimmy. When I got back to the house with you my wife was still lying on the floor unconscious. I had the witch come back and set the whole thing up to make it look like my wife had just gotten back from the hospital after giving birth to you. When she regained consciousness I told her she had passed out and I had taken her to the hospital. She believed every word. She asked what your name was and I told her, Ashlee. Spelled with two 'e's instead of 'ey'. I told her that she said the name in her unconscious state. Your mother wanted the names Ashlee and Jimmy so that's what I named you two. When I go on business trips I've been going to take care of Jimmy. My wife never suspected me."

He finally finished. I wasn't expecting that long of a story, then again I would have gotten mad if I would have gotten less. I looked over my shoulder and saw another shadow traveler.

"How do I look like my aunt?" I asked.

"Your mother and your aunt were twins. Having twins ran in the family." he said.

"Do you have any pictures of my mother?"

"No. Your aunt does though. Ask her if you can see them. But remember to ask . . ."

"If I can see pictures of my *aunt*. I got it. I better at this than you think."

"Speaking of that, how'd the fight go?"

I told him all the details of the fight. He would raise his eyebrows, widen his eyes, and flinch. When I was done he just stared at me.

"You did this without getting harmed? Yet, everyone else was injured in some way." he said confused.

"Yeah." I said it in a voice that told him he shouldn't be confused.

"Okay. I think they let you win. They let you live and they weren't trying to harm you. Although that makes no sense."

"No. Dad, it wasn't mercy that helped me win. Trust me, they didn't show any. It was my genes that helped me win."

"Your jeans?"

"Not my pants, dad. My genes. The science term."

"Oh. What gene are you talking about?"

"Have you ever heard of the fighting gene?"

"Well, yes. Everyone in our world has."

"I have it."

"You mean to tell me that your grandpa Phil was the carrier?"

"Yeah."

"Wait. Phil died. That means that you . . . you . . ."

"Surpassed him in skill? Yes, dad."

He shook his head. He must have realized that everything happens to me and that I hide a lot of things. I was able to hide the truth about my birth.

"We should go back to the house. Anything else you want to talk about before we do?" he said.

"No." I answered, looking away.

I had a feeling that my dad knew I was keeping something from him. Something important. He'd find out after Ryan and I graduate.

"Let's go home then." he whispered.

He put his arm around my shoulder and we walked back to the house to see my aunt. To see the pictures of my birth mother.

CHAPTER 22
Power

I had kept one of the pictures of my birth mother without my aunt realizing. I shoved it into my jacket pocket when she went to get more pictures. Even though she was my aunt, she was my mom. I grew up thinking she was my mom so it was weird finding out that she was my aunt. Now that I knew I kept picking things that were different between the two of us. She was more emotional than me. She had wavy hair, I had straight hair. She was moody sometimes and I was moody way more.

I didn't see how I had never realized. I guess I wanted to believe she was my mom so I did. Another thing that was a major difference was that she was cautious and I rushed into things without thinking. I was instinctional.

I lay across my bed most nights and stared at my mother's picture. She looked like she would be exactly like me. Crazy, random, and instinctional. I was thinking this one night when I heard a chuckle.

I jumped off my bed so fast that I got a headache.

"It's okay. It's just me."

Ryan.

I relaxed.

"Why can't you announce that you are here?" I sighed.

"Because even if I did that you would still freak out and give yourself a headache."

"Yeah, you're probably right."

"Probably?"

I shrugged and sat down on my bed. Ryan walked over and sat beside me. He put an arm around my shoulders. He looked at the picture that was still in my hands.

"Is that your birth mom?" he asked.

"Yeah." I said.

"You look exactly like her, you know?"

"Did I tell you that my mom and aunt were twins?"

"Yes."

"Okay. Did I tell you that having twins runs in the family?"

"Five times actually."

I blushed.

"Sorry. I need some sleep before school tomorrow though. I'm going to bed."

I crawled up to my pillows then turned and looked at him. He was staring at me with an odd expression. Like he thought I was crazy or something.

"What?" I asked.

"Tomorrow is the first day of our summer vacation."

"Oh. I guess I forgot."

"How could you possibly forget? You planned a trip to the beach for your family then your m-aunt asked me to come with you guys."

"Yeah. Like I said, I need sleep. G'night."

I lay down and covered up. I fell asleep almost instantly.

*   *   *

I woke up that morning and realized my picture was no longer in my hand. I started looking around on my bed then on the floor beside it. I tore up half of my room then finally found it next to Ryan.

He was sleeping in front of my computer. The computer was on the screen saver and my scanner was turned on. I reached over Ryan and clicked the mouse. He had Photoshop opened. He had been editing the picture of my mother. I was now in it standing beside her. He had also added affects to make it look good, fixed the contrast and lighting so the cutout of me matched the original picture. He had the printing options box up so I figured he was done with it. I looked at the printer where there was photo paper.

He had edited the picture to make me feel better. But somehow it didn't. It just seemed a little off now.

Ryan snored. I took the picture of my mom and put it on my bedside table. Then I cleaned the part of my room that I had demolished. I turned to face Ryan but he wasn't in front of the computer anymore. I looked around the room but he wasn't there. The bathroom door opened and Ryan walked out. He glanced at me and blushed.

"Sorry. Were you looking for me?" he said.

"Yeah. So I could tell you to go home and sleep." I told him.

"I'm fine."

"As much as you hate it, you need to sleep. You're not immune to it like you think you are."

"Fine. I'll go home and sleep. You can print that picture if you want it."

"Thanks for making the picture."

He nodded and walked over to the window. I followed him and looked down at the ladder. When I did I saw a shadow traveler. They seemed to be watching everyone.

"Ashlee? Can I use your computer for a second?" Ryan asked distractedly.

"Yeah, sure, go ahead." I said.

He walked over to the computer and got on the internet. In the search box he typed in 'shadow traveler'. The one result that I had gotten last time popped up. He clicked on it. The picture of the tree line popped up at the top of the page. He scrolled down to the part about the powerful necromancer bringing the shadow travelers back. He clicked on that paragraph and it took him to a different web site. Something I hadn't noticed before.

It was a site about the necromancer that would bring the shadow travelers back. The only pictures on this web site were disturbing pictures of the dead rising from cracks in the ground.

"That's what they are doing." Ryan said.

"Excuse me?" I said confused.

"The shadow travelers aren't spying on us. They are looking for Cole."

"Why?"

"Because he is the one that brought them back. He is their new leader."

"New leader?"

"Whoever brings them back is destined to be their leader. Cole brought them back; he is their leader. He is the last necromancer."

"That must suck to be the last of something."

"Just a little. No one can help him learn how to use his powers. We've never met another necromancer. Reading those necromancy books is the only way he learns."

"Wow. He's pretty good for just reading books on the stuff."

Ryan nodded and crawled out the window and onto the ladder. He looked back in the window at me.

"I'll tell them I can take them to Cole." he said.

"They won't understand you." I told him.

I didn't even know how I knew that.

"What do you mean?" Ryan asked.

"Only a necromancer can communicate with them. They won't understand you because they have their own language."

"And you think that Cole knows their language?"

"Yes. In his subconscious. Kind of like how I know this stuff."

"Okay. Can I bring him by here later? The shadow travelers seem to stay where you are more than anywhere else. I think they are attracted to all the power you radiate."

"The power I radiate?"

"Yeah. When you are really powerful the power will kind of project. It's to warn others not to mess with you."

"Has my power always done that?"

"No. It started when you realized who you were. When you found out you had the gene and that you were the child in the prophecy. It radiated even more when you surpassed your grandfather. And more at his funeral after the Royal told you the entire prophecy."

"And it just gradually projects more and more everyday now, I'm guessing. Correct me if I'm wrong."

"You're not wrong. You're exactly right. When Alexander sees you next you will be even more powerful than the Royals. And you know what that part at the end of the prophecy meant, right?"

"'*She shall choose to rule or destroy.*' What do you think it means?"

"I know exactly what it means. You have to either overthrow the Royals or let the Royals continue ruling and basically destroy the human race so that there are only supernaturals. There have been rumors that they have been planning this for hundreds of years. The prophecy just confirms it."

"Hundreds of years?"

"The Royals are immortal. They never die unless they are overthrown."

Ryan looked over his shoulder then started down the ladder. I watched him until he reached the ground. Then I turned to face my empty room. Only one problem: it wasn't empty.

Karla was sitting on my bed waiting for me. I walked over and sat down beside her.

"I got bored at Grace's house." she said.

"How did you get in here?" I asked her.

"I turned invisible when your dad walked out. He left the door open so I just slipped right in."

"You turned invisible?"

"Yeah. I just learned I could do that. Your dad walked out of the house so I freaked and stood really still. He almost walked into me so I looked down. I couldn't even see my body. It was *so* cool!"

"That's really weird. Is that because you are a reborn spirit and you have some type of ghost powers?"

"That's what I thought. I wanted to ask Cole but then I realized I had no idea where he lived. So I just came to ask you."

"Cole's going to come over with Ryan sometime later. You can just wait around here if you want."

"Sounds good to me."

"Does Grace know that you left? Or will she think that you got kidnapped?"

"Ha ha. You are *so* funny. No, I told her."

"Just trying to help my sister *not* freak out."

She laughed for real that time. As soon as she did my stomach growled and she laughed even harder. I put my hand over her mouth.

"Karla! Quiet!" I whispered.

"Sorry!" she choked between my fingers and spurts of laughter.

I laughed quietly at her. When she had calmed down enough I let go of her mouth. I stood and walked to the door. Then I remembered Karla couldn't really stay here very long.

"You can either stay up here while I eat or turn invisible and come eat with me." I told her.

"I'll come down with you, but how will I eat?"

"I'll hold out my food when my parents aren't looking."

"Alright then. To the kitchen!"

She disappeared. I walked out the door and left it wide open for her. I realized that, if I really concentrated, I could see her as a slight shimmer that could be mistaken as a glare from the sun.

We ran down to the kitchen. My aunt had my plate fixed like she had known I would be down.

"Hi dear." my aunt said as I sat down, "Did you hear that your father doesn't have to go on business trips anymore. He has a more important job now that doesn't involve traveling."

"That's great mom!" I said.

My voice wavered on the word 'mom.'

"Oh. Your father wants to talk to you before you eat. He is upstairs in his study." she told me, ignoring my wavering.

"Um, I thought he didn't want Duke and me to ever go in his study?" I said confused.

"Usually. But he said he needs to talk to you about something important. So you go straight up there."

"Okay."

I turned and left the room. I saw, out of the corner of my eye, the shimmer-Karla hesitate. As I got farther away she ran after me. She followed me to the door of my dad's study then grabbed my arm. I couldn't see her but I knew what she was going to ask.

"Do you want me to stay out here?" she asked.

I shook my head and she let go of my arm.

I knocked on the door and my dad told me to come in. I opened the door and let Karla in first. It looked like I was hesitating in the doorway, not letting an invisible person in the room. I walked in behind her and strode across the room to stand in front of my dad's desk. He nodded to the chair behind me and I sat.

He sat forward, locked his hands, and rested his chin on them. He looked me over a couple times then smiled.

"I went to see Jimmy today." he announced.

"Yeah?" I asked.

"Yes. He spoke very highly of you. He also told me about how you are destined to either rule or destroy the supernatural world."

"Oh."

"Yeah, 'oh.' Why didn't you tell me that when you first got here?"

"I try not to think about it too much. I don't really like the fact that I decide the fate of the supernatural world."

"I kind of understand. I would be the same."

"And by the way, I have someone to show you."

"Some*one*?"

"Yeah. Hey, Karla? Turn visible."

"Karla?"

Karla appeared at my side and my dad nearly had a heart attack. I felt bad about that, but he needed to know that Karla was back.

"Hi, Mr. Teaford." she said politely and shyly.

"Hi, Karla . . ." my father said staring at her.

CHAPTER 23
Not Alone

Ryan and Cole were sitting on the ground in my backyard. Karla and I were watching them from the patio. Cole was speaking in the language of the shadow travelers. It was a clicking sort of language and it sounded weird coming from Cole's mouth.

Ryan looked back at Karla and me and motioned for us to come over. We walked slowly toward them. Cole nodded to us but kept talking to the shadow traveler sitting in front of him.

Cole pointed to me and said something to the shadow traveler. Then he did the same with Karla. Introducing us. I nodded to the dark figure and so did Karla. It nodded back and resumed talking to Cole.

After a while, the shadow traveler stood and disappeared, along with all the others that were in my yard. Cole turned to us.

"I told them to go spy on Alex." he said.

I nodded.

"They are very obedient." he added.

"Of course they are. They are here to serve you now." Ryan told him.

"Yeah. That's kind of how I felt when he brought me back." Karla admitted, "The urge to serve him. I ignored it though because I don't serve anyone but God."

"That's understandable. You've died and came back. It only makes sense."

I looked over at my gate. I really wanted to just run out of it screaming. I didn't want any part of this weird, powerful life. I just wanted to be normal. I wanted things to be like when I was still human, before Alexander changed me. Then again, I was never meant to be normal.

Ryan sighed sadly and grabbed my hand. He had been reading my mind.

"So we have the shadow travelers on our side. We have Cole and he can raise the dead. Do we really need an army?" I said.

Ryan and Cole looked at each other.

"The dead will only fight in the company of the living." Cole told me.

"Why?"

"It's just their way."

I nodded.

Now we had to gather another army. More people dying because of us. Then I had to rule or destroy. I didn't want to destroy so I had no choice but to rule. To rule I had to overthrow the Royals which no one has done. Or tried.

"It will be okay. We are here to help you. You don't have to fulfill the prophecy alone." Ryan said squeezing my hand.

The others nodded.

I loved them all. I didn't want them to get hurt. Even if I told them no they wouldn't listen. They were so committed. I smiled at each of them and they smiled back.

We would win. Everything.